Previously on the Accidental Blast-off

Thank you for buying *Nanny Piggins and the Accidental Blast-off*. You have made an excellent purchasing decision! Don't worry if you have not read the previous books in the series. Each one of Nanny Piggins' adventures is a riveting tale in its own right, so you don't have to read them in any particular order.

But if you don't believe me, I will now give you a quick summary of everything that has happened so far . . .

It all started when Nanny Piggins (the world's most glamorous flying pig) ran away from the circus and took up a job as the Green's nanny. The Green children, Derrick, Samantha and Michael, fell in love with her instantly. Who could not fall in love with a nanny who thinks she has found the cure to the common cold – lemon cake.

Before long Nanny Piggins' brother, Boris the dancing bear, came to live in the Green's garden shed, although Mr Green (the father) still hasn't realised he is there because Boris is very good at disguising himself.

And that's all you need to know. There are a lot of other characters – a wicked Ringmaster, thirteen identical twin sisters, a nasty neighbour, a nice neighbour, a retired army colonel, a very silly headmaster, a hygiene-obsessed rival nanny and the two very clean children she looks after (Samson and Margaret Wallace) – but you will pick all that up as you go along.

So now all you have to do is fix yourself a lovely cakey chocolatey snack, find a comfortable place to curl up and enjoy the latest instalment of Nanny Piggins' wonderful adventures.

Best wishes and happy reading,
R. A. Spratt, the author

Nanny Piggins

AND THE ACCIDENTAL BLAST-OFF

BOOK 4

R. A. SPRATT

RANDOM HOUSE AUSTRALIA

To Charlotte, Finlay and Fergus

A Random House book
Published by Random House Australia Pty Ltd
Level 3, 100 Pacific Highway, North Sydney NSW 2060
www.randomhouse.com.au

First published by Random House Australia in 2011
This edition published by Random House Australia in 2012

Addresses for companies within the Random House Group can be found at
www.randomhouse.com.au/offices

National Library of Australia
Cataloguing-in-Publication Entry

Author: Spratt, R. A.
Title: Nanny Piggins and the Accidental Blast-off
Edition: 2nd ed.
ISBN: 978 1 74275 368 3
Series: Nanny Piggins; 4.
Target Audience: For primary school age
Dewey Number: A823.4

Cover illustration by Gypsy Taylor
Cover design by Christabella Designs
Internal design by Jobi Murphy
Internal illustrations by R. A. Spratt
Typeset in Adobe Garamond by Midland Typesetters, Australia
Printed in Australia by Griffin Press, an Accredited ISO AS/NZS 14001:2004
Environmental Management System printer.

CONTENTS

Chapter 1
Nanny Piggins and the Company Picnic............1

Chapter 2
Nanny Piggins and the Truancy Officer...........24

Chapter 3
Nanny Piggins and the Accidental Blast-off.......46

Chapter 4
Nanny Piggins and the Giant Lollipop............75

Chapter 5
Coach Green....................................100

Chapter 6
Nanny Piggins Stands Accused 128

Chapter 7
Boris the Big Bad Bear 157

Chapter 8
Nanny Piggins: Steel Chef.......................182

Chapter 9
Nanny Piggins Saves Christmas...................210

Chapter 10
Nanny Piggins Turns a Lemon into
Lemonade..234

CHAPTER 1

Nanny Piggins and the Company Picnic

Nanny Piggins and the children were sitting at the dining table having a very unpleasant meal. There was nothing wrong with the food. (In Nanny Piggins' opinion you should never blame food for your problems, it would be like blaming a rainbow for the rain.) The problem was that Mr Green was sitting at the head of the table. Their father's presence had the effect of sucking the fun out of just about any situation. And on this occasion it could not be avoided because it was Father's Day.

Now Mr Green did not want to celebrate Father's Day any more than his children did. But he had to because he'd got in trouble the previous year when the senior partner at the law firm where he worked had caught him eating his Father's Day dinner in the office. Isabella Dunkhurst had been horrified that a man with three children would rather eat a soggy cheese sandwich at his desk than go home to his family. She had told him off thoroughly (and having been a practising lawyer for thirty years she was very good at telling people off. She knew lots of big words for 'idiot' and 'naughty') and threatened to dock his pay if he did not go home immediately.

This year Mr Green had raced home as soon as the clock struck 5 pm. He lived in such fear and awe of Isabella Dunkhurst that he dared not displease her twice in a twelve-month period.

The children had done the right thing and bought their father presents (even though he was the least deserving father, possibly in the entire world). And surprisingly Mr Green had actually been grateful and almost touched to receive a pair of socks, a bottle of aftershave and a book about the weather. Because you see, the children had included the receipts in the packages (they knew their father well), so he would be able to return the presents the next day and get the money. And Mr Green loved nothing more than money.

And so Nanny Piggins and the children were just forcing down the horrible broccoli stew that Mr Green had insisted he was given as his Father's Day treat (he had read that there was a glut of broccoli in Nigeria, which was causing that vegetable to be very cheap. Fortunately Nanny Piggins had the foresight to make the children chocolate-coated waffles as a late afternoon snack, so they were unlikely to starve or die of broccoli poisoning) when suddenly the silence was interrupted by a loud knock at the front door.

'Who could that be?' demanded Mr Green. 'Don't they know it's Father's Day?'

'Perhaps it's someone from your work come to check that you're actually here,' suggested Nanny Piggins.

Mr Green recoiled in fear. 'Don't answer the door,' he said.

'Then they'll definitely think you're not here,' reasoned Nanny Piggins.

'Answer it, quick, one of you answer it!' insisted Mr Green.

Derrick, being the eldest, stood up and hurried out of the room.

'I haven't done anything wrong this year, have I?' asked Mr Green. And actually, he had not. But he had certainly not *wanted* to come home for Father's Day, and he was worried that his employers had found some way to read his thoughts.

A few moments later, when Isabella Dunkhurst, the firm's senior partner, actually did walk in through the dining room door, Mr Green looked like he was going to drop dead of a heart attack and burst into tears all at once.

'I'm here, I'm here,' protested Mr Green. 'I swear I haven't done any work all evening.'

'Then what are those figures you've jotted on your napkin?' asked Samantha, whose keen eyesight had spotted the sums her father had secretly been doing under the tablecloth, as he worked out how a client who made a fortune pumping toxic waste into the ocean could get his money offshore before the dead fish started washing up onshore.

'I'm not here about that,' said Isabella Dunkhurst.

'You're not?' asked Mr Green, sighing with relief.

'Although hand me the napkin, I'll give it to the accounts department tomorrow so they know to dock his pay,' added Isabella Dunkhurst.

'Why are you here then?' asked Michael.

'To see Nanny Piggins,' explained Isabella Dunkhurst.

'Really?' said Nanny Piggins and the children, all equally surprised.

'Are you going to arrest her?' asked Mr Green hopefully.

'No, I'm going to thank her,' said Isabella Dunkhurst.

'What for?' asked Nanny Piggins. She was used to people being desperately grateful to her, but that was usually when she had given them a slice of cake. And Nanny Piggins could not remember giving Isabella Dunkhurst a slice of cake.

'Do you remember when you came to the firm's annual dinner and taught us all how to tap dance?' asked Isabella Dunkhurst.

Nanny Piggins rubbed her snout as she wracked her memory. 'No, but I do so many astounding things I sometimes lose track.'

'You remember,' said Derrick. 'Father took you as his date.'

'I did not!' protested Mr Green.

'You wore your sequined gown with the peacock feathers and fairy-light headdress,' Samantha reminded her.

Nanny Piggins shook her head. 'Still doesn't ring a bell.'

'They served orange poppyseed cake,' reminded Michael.

'I remember it precisely!' exclaimed Nanny Piggins. 'It was delicious! I ate eight or nine slices. Have you brought me some more?'

'No, I'm afraid not,' admitted Isabella Dunkhurst.

'Never mind, I can whip some up myself later,' said Nanny Piggins, 'but I remember it all now. After licking the last of the cake off my plate, I borrowed a packet of drawing pins from the head waiter, stuck them in my shoes and taught you all how to tap dance like Fred Astaire.'

'It was the most wonderful night of my life,' gushed Isabella Dunkhurst.

'Really?' said the children, amazed.

'I told you it was jolly good cake,' said Nanny Piggins.

'No, not the cake,' said Isabella Dunkhurst. 'The tap dancing lesson! It inspired me. I have been taking tap dancing lessons seven days a week ever since.'

'Tap is a wonderful form of dance,' said Boris. (He was hidden behind the curtains because Mr Green still did not realise that the world's greatest ballet dancing bear was living in his garden shed.) 'Tap dancing combines the grace of ballet with the joy of banging saucepans together.'

'Your curtain is quite right,' agreed Isabella Dunkhurst, 'I just love it, which is why I have decided to leave the firm.'

'What?!' exclaimed Mr Green, leaping from his seat. He was so horrified at the prospect of losing Isabella Dunkhurst from his life that his eyes started to water and his chin began to quiver. And you have to understand that Mr Green did not even cry when his own mother left him. (She abandoned him at a train station on Mother's Day to run off with the milkman. Which is not anywhere near as sad a story as it sounds, because Mr Green was thirty-seven years old at the time and the only reason she ran away was because she could not get him to leave home.)

'You can't, you can't leave me,' protested Mr Green.

Everyone in the room looked at Mr Green for a moment, collectively decided it was best to ignore him and continued on with their conversation.

'I have decided to leave the firm to become a tap-dancing lawyer,' explained Isabella Dunkhurst. She positively glowed with happiness as she revealed her decision.

'What does a tap-dancing lawyer do?' asked Michael.

'Do you go into court and tap dance around the other barristers' legal arguments?' asked Derrick.

'Oh no, that would be silly,' said Isabella Dunkhurst. 'No, I dance on a stage like a normal tap dancer. Then people from the crowd call out their problems and I give them legal advice.'

'It sounds wonderful,' said Nanny Piggins. 'I love going to the theatre and I often get into legal trouble. It would be so convenient to be able to combine enjoying a first-rate night of dance with getting some top-notch legal arguments to yell at the Police Sergeant the next day.'

'You'll have to come along to a show,' said Isabella Dunkhurst.

'Oh we will, I'm sure it won't be long before I get into some legal difficulty,' said Nanny Piggins. 'Any day now Mr Mahmood could discover the hole I accidentally burnt in his hedge.'

'Well I'll go and let you enjoy the rest of your Father's Day,' said Isabella Dunkhurst. 'I just wanted to thank you for turning my life around and making me see that there was more to life than telling off a bunch of boring old lawyers every day.'

Mr Green, who had been weeping quietly in the corner this whole time, now let out a wail of despair.

'What's wrong with him?' asked Isabella. 'Should he be on medication?'

'I've tried medicating him with cake,' admitted Nanny Piggins, 'but the sugar only makes him even more boring.'

'What will I do without you?' wailed Mr Green.

'But I only see you once or twice a month to tell you off for being amoral,' said Isabella Dunkhurst.

'It is the highlight of my month,' blubbered Mr Green.

'Pull yourself together, man,' scolded Isabella. 'There will be a new senior partner starting on Monday. I'm sure it won't take him long to get the measure of you. He'll be tearing strips off you within a fortnight.'

'Oh I hope so, I do hope so,' sobbed Mr Green.

That Monday was the first time Nanny Piggins and the children had ever waited excitedly for Mr Green to come home (if you do not count the time they put a skunk in his bed). They could not wait to find out if the new senior partner would sack Mr Green. Or worse, revoke his executive bathroom privileges. (Mr Green hated using the same bathroom as the boys from the mailroom, because they insisted on making jovial small talk about football teams.)

When Mr Green came into sight, trudging up the street, it appeared their predictions had come true. He looked so miserable. His face was ashen and he walked as though his shoes were made of lead. Nanny Piggins and the children actually began to feel a little bit sorry for him.

'Is everything all right, Father?' asked Samantha as he slumped into an armchair.

'The worst has happened,' muttered Mr Green, clearly distraught.

'The new senior partner sacked you?' asked Derrick.

'I wish he would,' wailed Mr Green. 'No, it's much much worse. He is holding a . . .' Mr Green paused here as he struggled to hold back tears, '. . . a company picnic.'

'What's wrong with that?' asked Nanny Piggins.

'Everybody has to take their families!' explained Mr Green, showing them the written invitation.

'Noooooo!' said the three Green children, as equally horrified as their father.

'The new senior partner believes in modern management techniques,' moaned Mr Green. 'He prioritises family values and a work/life balance.'

'What does that mean?' asked Nanny Piggins.

'I don't know but it sounds awful,' complained Mr Green.

'You poor thing,' sympathised Nanny Piggins. 'And I suppose someone ratted you out and told him you have three children.'

'Yes, Smythe from accounts dobbed me in,' admitted Mr Green. 'He's never forgiven me for borrowing his stapler without asking'.

'It'll be all right,' said Nanny Piggins. 'Picnics are a lot of fun. Food eaten outdoors tastes even better than food eaten indoors. And I can arrange some good picnic games if you like.'

'You will not!' exclaimed Mr Green, leaping to his feet. 'It's bad enough that I am being forced to take my children to a work-related social function. There's no way I'm taking a pig as well. What will people say?'

'"Look at that poor pig, imagine having to go to

a picnic with him",' guessed Nanny Piggins (accurately).

'I won't stand for it,' declared Mr Green. 'I forbid you to come within 500 metres of the picnic site.'

'Really?' said Nanny Piggins, her eyes narrowing. It was always a terrible mistake when Mr Green forbade her to do anything. Pretty much the only way of guaranteeing Nanny Piggins would do something was to forbid her to do it.

'But it says on the invitation that you have to bring a plate of food,' read Samantha. 'You can't cook that yourself.'

'She's right,' agreed Michael. 'You can't make toast without having to fetch a golf club and smash the smoke detector down from the ceiling.'

'And you know Nanny Piggins is the best cook in the country,' said Derrick.

Nanny Piggins coughed.

'Sorry, I meant to say the best cook in the entire world,' amended Derrick.

Nanny Piggins nodded. The boy was only telling the truth.

'That's not your concern,' said Mr Green, rudely snatching the invitation back. 'I'll just hire a chef.'

Nanny Piggins did not say anything further on the subject but the children knew their father was in terrible trouble because of the way she glowered at him. She was clearly making plans.

When the morning of the picnic arrived, Mr Green made Derrick, Samantha and Michael line up in the hallway so he could inspect them as he marked off a checklist. 'Clothes starched, check. Shoes shined, check. Nanny safely in house . . .' Mr Green looked at Nanny Piggins. He knew his nanny was a master of disguise. But there was no way an imposter could imitate the glare of loathing she was giving him now. 'Check.' He put the clipboard away. 'All right, as soon as the chef arrives with the plate of crudités we can leave.'

'What's crudités?' Michael whispered to Nanny Piggins.

'It's just a fancy word for snacks,' explained Nanny Piggins.

The doorbell rang.

'That will be him now,' said Mr Green, throwing open the front door. But he recoiled in shock because there was no gourmet French chef standing on his doorstep. Just a small boy. And Mr Green had an instinctive revulsion towards all children (not just his own).

'Go away. I'm waiting for an important chef,' said Mr Green, his foot twitching with the urge to give the child a kick.

'I've come with a message from chef Jean-Luc,' said the boy. 'He said to say that –' the boy took a crumpled piece of paper from his pocket and read – 'he couldn't make your crudités because he's had to make a sudden and unexpected trip to Bolivia.'

'What?' exploded Mr Green.

The boy had the good sense to make a run for it at this point.

Mr Green slammed the door shut, then turned to glare at Nanny Piggins. 'You had something to do with this, didn't you?' he accused.

Nanny Piggins smiled. She had never looked more innocent in her life, so the children immediately knew she was guilty.

'I don't know what you mean,' said Nanny Piggins.

'Don't you have an aunt in Bolivia?' asked Mr Green.

'I do,' conceded Nanny Piggins, 'but if she had some sort of French cuisine-related emergency that urgently required her to fly over a top chef, I'm sure there's no way you could prove that had anything to do with me.'

Mr Green glowered at her and Nanny Piggins smiled back. 'I do hope the senior partner won't think badly of you if you turn up empty-handed,' said Nanny Piggins.

'I'll pick something up at the shops,' countered Mr Green.

'The shops are closed because it's Sunday afternoon,' said Derrick.

'What a shame,' said Nanny Piggins. 'If only a world-famous cooking pig was nearby. One that you had *not* been extremely rude to.'

They all stared at Mr Green. He looked like his head was going to explode with rage, because he knew he was now going to have to negotiate with Nanny Piggins. And he never did well when they negotiated.

'How much chocolate cake will I have to give you for you to agree to make a plate of crudités to take to the picnic?' he asked in the calmest and most reasonable voice his rage would allow.

'Hmmm,' said Nanny Piggins as she considered the question. 'No, today I don't feel like cake.'

The children gasped. They had never heard Nanny Piggins utter such shocking words before.

'Today I feel like picnic food,' said Nanny Piggins with a mischievous glint in her eye.

'What are you saying?' asked Mr Green, fearing the worst.

'I will make you a plate of food, and something much better than crudités,' said Nanny Piggins, 'but only if you take me to the picnic with you.'

Mr Green considered his limited options. 'Will you agree not to speak to anyone?'

'No,' said Nanny Piggins.

'Will you agree not to take part in any games?' asked Mr Green.

'No,' said Nanny Piggins.

'Will you at least agree not to teach any of the partners how to dance or sing or perform circus tricks of any kind?' begged Mr Green.

'I'll try,' conceded Nanny Piggins, 'but I can't make any promises. I'm a natural teacher. When I see people desperately in need of instruction it's instinctive for me to take them in hand.'

Mr Green looked defeated.

'You really don't have any choice, Father,' said Michael.

'All right. How long will it take you to whip something up?' Mr Green asked.

'Let me see,' said Nanny Piggins, disappearing into the kitchen. She returned one second later holding a huge five-tiered tea-tray laden with the most exquisitely delicious tea cakes. 'Oh look, I just happened to have this lying around in the kitchen.'

Mr Green started to go red in the face. (If this had been a court of law he could have entered the tea cakes as evidence, proving just how much advance knowledge she must have had of the chef's sudden and unexpected need to visit Bolivia.)

'We should get going,' urged Derrick, thinking it best if they all went to the picnic before his father engaged Nanny Piggins in another argument he would be sure to lose.

When they neared the picnic ground, Nanny Piggins and the children started to get excited. They could see colourful bunting strung between the trees, trestle tables packed with food, great big barrels of fresh homemade lemonade and all sorts of equipment set out for the after-lunch games. The new senior partner obviously knew how to throw a party. Even the weather was perfect. It was sunny but not too hot, just right for outdoor fun. Nanny Piggins and the children were twitching to get out of the car as Mr Green slowly and over-cautiously reverse-parked his Rolls Royce, pulling it in and out of the parking space several times.

Nanny Piggins was just about to leap out and sprint towards the food table when Mr Green flicked on the central locking so no-one could escape.

'What are you doing?' demanded Nanny Piggins, desperately shaking the door handle. 'Can't you see the food!'

'The food isn't going anywhere,' said Mr Green.

'Yes it is!' exclaimed Nanny Piggins. 'It'll go in other people's mouths if we don't get there first.'

Mr Green just ignored her and launched into a speech. 'Before we join the picnic I want all of you to give me your assurance that you will behave in an exemplary manner for the duration of the picnic and particularly in the vicinity of my co-workers . . .'

Unfortunately Mr Green made the mistake of closing his eyes while making this speech and when he opened them it was to see Nanny Piggins, Derrick and Samantha standing on top of his car as they pulled Michael up through the sunroof.

'Quick, run for it!' urged Nanny Piggins. And the four of them bolted for the food.

What followed was a horrible afternoon for Mr Green. When you are not very good at having fun yourself, there is nothing worse than watching all your most loathed colleagues have the best afternoon of their lives. Particularly when it is thanks to the impossibly glamorous pig you brought along with you.

After eating half the food on the trestle table (Nanny Piggins graciously left some for the other picnic goers), Nanny Piggins turned her attention to the games. Picnic games were just the sort of thing she excelled at.

She easily won the sack race, having perfected her sack-jumping technique the time the Ringmaster bundled her up and shipped her to outer Mongolia. It had taken her four days to hop from Uzbekistan to Kurdistan, so she had lots of experience.

Nanny Piggins also won the egg and spoon race, because, again, she was such a practised hand. Many was the time, in her excitement to bake a cake, she had the batter half mixed before she realised she had run out of eggs, then had to sprint to the shop and back with a fresh carton. (The children had often wondered why she always balanced the carton on a spoon, but now they were glad she did.)

Nanny Piggins even won the three-legged race, which was no easy feat. Being four foot tall, her legs were very short. Also, she was competing with Mr

Green (the new senior partner insisted everyone take part). But Nanny Piggins did not let Mr Green slow her down. She had become very good at dragging a dead weight the time she pulled the Ringmaster's caravan into a swollen creek to teach him a lesson about not providing chocolate biscuits for his staff. So as soon as the starter's pistol fired she took off like a rocket, dragging Mr Green around the obstacle course with all the care and consideration she would give a sack of potatoes (and Nanny Piggins had very little care or consideration for potatoes).

After the official games were over Nanny Piggins persuaded everyone to go down to the creek for a water fight, which Nanny Piggins won when she filled up the punch bowl and tipped it over the new senior partner's head.

Then, as a special treat, Nanny Piggins did an impromptu medley of folk songs from every country she had ever been to, with accompanying dances and fire breathing where appropriate (and even more enjoyably, where it was not appropriate).

So when the sun began to dip below the trees and everyone was exhausted from so much fresh air and fun (even Mr Green was exhausted, but in his case, from wanting to go home), the Senior Partner climbed up on an apple crate.

He was a surprisingly handsome man for a lawyer. His eyes crinkled when he smiled, which he did a lot, as well as winking and clapping people on the back. Altogether he looked and sounded more like a rugby coach. But while he was very jovial, there was a glint in his eye as though he might just do something unexpected, like crash tackle you to the ground. So naturally he commanded respect.

'Thank you all for coming to this wonderful family picnic,' began the Senior Partner. 'We should make this an annual event!'

Everyone cheered except Mr Green, who groaned.

'Now it's time for me to announce the King and Queen of the picnic,' continued the Senior Partner, 'but one picnic goer has been so much fun, I think she deserves to be King *and* Queen. So I'm going to give her both crowns. Nanny Piggins, these are for you.'

Nanny Piggins stepped forward and the Senior Partner put both crowns on her head.

'Your athleticism in the games was awesome, your tea cakes were delicious and I'm sure we're all grateful that you taught us how to yodel,' continued the Senior Partner. 'I, for one, am going to book myself in for more yodelling lessons as soon as I get home.'

Everyone applauded except Mr Green, who groaned again. This time he actually was in physical pain.

'Would you like to say a few words?' asked the Senior Partner.

'Oh no,' begged Mr Green.

'Yes, I would,' said Nanny Piggins, climbing up onto the apple crate. 'I'd just like to say I had a lovely time. You were all much less boring than I thought a bunch of lawyers would be.'

Everyone laughed (which surprised Nanny Piggins because she was not joking).

'All right, it's time to head home,' said the Senior Partner. 'I expect to see you bright and early at the office tomorrow. But before we go, I have one more announcement. I arranged this picnic because I think families are so important.'

Mr Green rolled his eyes and shuddered.

'But,' continued the Senior Partner, 'I know some of you men out there sometimes put too much emphasis on work. That is why I have decided to hold a Father of the Year Competition. And you all have to enter – that's an order!' For a moment the twinkle in the Senior Partner's eye was replaced with a steely resolve, but then he smiled again. 'Over the next few months I want you to show me what good fathers you are. Then the winner will be awarded a special prize. A crystal trophy.'

Mr Green gasped. He loved crystal trophies. It made him feel so important to have one on his desk.

'And . . .' continued the Senior Partner, 'something really good, which I haven't decided on yet!'

Everyone applauded. The men immediately started eyeing each other up and convincing themselves that while they may not be good fathers, all the others were a lot worse than them.

And so, after the trestle tables and picnic games were packed away, Nanny Piggins and the Green family drove home. The three children were blissfully happy, having had a wonderful day of food, fun and watching their father squirm. Nanny Piggins was delighted to have another two crowns to add to her jewellery box (she had built up quite a collection over the years). Only Mr Green was sad at the prospect of having to pretend to be a good father, at least for the foreseeable future.

CHAPTER 2

Nanny Piggins and the Truancy Officer

Nanny Piggins and the children were sitting on the naughty bench outside the headmaster's office. It was unusual for a parent or guardian to be sent to sit on this much-feared piece of furniture, but in Nanny Piggins' case they had made an exception.

The children anxiously fidgeted and fretted, but the situation did not seem to bother Nanny Piggins in the slightest. Her trotters swung happily above the floor as they waited to be summoned by Headmaster Pimplestock. And they had been waiting for a while because he had locked himself in his office so he could think up some really cutting things to say.

'We're going to be in so much trouble,' worried Samantha. She was not a girl who was given to biting her fingernails. But as she sat on the naughty bench (a piece of furniture in her mind associated with the greatest level of sin – like mugging old ladies, or handing your homework in a week late), she seriously considered taking the habit up, just to give herself something to do.

'Pish!' said Nanny Piggins. 'There's nothing he can do to us. Schools haven't been allowed to sentence children to hard labour for years. At least I'm pretty sure that's the case.'

The door suddenly swung open and Headmaster Pimplestock stood glaring at them. He had straightened his tie and combed his hair in an effort to look intimidating.

'Nanny Piggins, I'll see you now,' announced Headmaster Pimplestock, trying (and failing) to sound dignified and important.

They followed the headmaster into his office. He had taken away the chairs that usually sat opposite the desk so Nanny Piggins would not be able to sit down and be comfortable (or climb up on the chair and attack him, as she had on her previous visit when Headmaster Pimplestock told her that the lamington drive had run out of lamingtons).

'Hello, Headmaster, how are you today?' asked Nanny Piggins jauntily.

The headmaster scowled, trying to express the gravity of the situation with his facial features. 'This is a very serious matter,' he said. 'Very serious indeed.'

'Is it?' asked Nanny Piggins, baffled.

'I have just had a phone call from the hospital,' announced Headmaster Pimplestock.

Samantha whimpered. Michael clutched his nanny's hand.

Headmaster Pimplestock paused for dramatic emphasis as he glared at each of the Green children in turn, then Nanny Piggins (he did not glare at her too long because she was smiling at him in a disarming way).

'And the hospital says,' he continued, 'that the truancy officer will be all right.'

The three children breathed a sigh of relief.

'I thought so,' said Nanny Piggins.

'Although, apparently, psychological damage has been done,' said Headmaster Pimplestock.

'Now are you sure that wasn't a pre-existing problem?' asked Nanny Piggins. To her mind, you would have to be insane to want to become a truancy officer in the first place.

'The fact remains,' said Headmaster Pimple-stock, starting to use some of the phrases he had practised, 'that you wilfully lied to this institution when you rang up and claimed that Derrick, Samantha and Michael all had convection-inhibited sunspots.'

'But they did,' protested Nanny Piggins.

'Convection-inhibited sunspots are meteorological phenomena, not symptoms of a human disease!' accused Headmaster Pimplestock.

'Which is why I was so alarmed when they got them,' said Nanny Piggins, using her most wide-eyed innocent expression.

'And I put it to you,' continued Headmaster Pimplestock (now he was using expressions he had picked up from watching courtroom dramas on TV), 'that you knew full well that Truancy Officer Britches was following you when you decided to enter that swamp.'

'We weren't going to let the fact that she is such a shocking busybody alter our plans for the day,' protested Nanny Piggins.

'Nanny Piggins planned to take us frog catching long before we knew the truancy officer was after us,' confirmed Derrick.

'So you admit that you weren't sick at all!' declared Headmaster Pimplestock. 'You had planned this day trip into the swamp in advance.'

'Everyone knows that fresh air and alluvial mud are the best cure for sunspots,' argued Nanny Piggins. 'I took the children frog catching purely for medicinal reasons.'

The frog in Michael's lunch box ribbited its agreement.

'Speaking of which, we really should be getting our frogs home,' chided Nanny Piggins. 'The truancy officer might be all right, but it would be terrible if there was a frog fatality.'

Headmaster Pimplestock was starting to sense the telling-off was slipping away from him. The cleverly worded denunciations escaped him and he degenerated to wild accusations. 'The fact remains that you endangered the truancy officer's life by leading her into a swamp where she was attacked by a crocodile!'

'Yes, but then we saved her from the crocodile, didn't we?' said Nanny Piggins.

'Nanny Piggins was really brave when she leapt on the crocodile's back,' argued Michael.

'And shoved a big chocolate cake in its mouth before it could bite the truancy officer,' added Samantha.

'Then wrestled the handle of her handbag over its jaws so it couldn't bite anybody else,' described Derrick.

'I thought it showed great personal sacrifice,' agreed Nanny Piggins, 'because that was a very nice handbag, whereas the truancy officer is not nice at all.'

'I can see you are totally unrepentant,' denounced Headmaster Pimplestock.

'You're right, I am,' admitted Nanny Piggins. (She might not obey the attendance rules but she was not a liar.)

'Well, you have left me no choice,' said Headmaster Pimplestock. He allowed himself a smirk here because he had another trick up his sleeve. 'This morning, head office sent over a new truancy officer.'

'I hope this one can swim,' said Nanny Piggins.

'I'd like you meet Mr Bernard!' said Headmaster Pimplestock.

With that the door opened and a man entered the room. (I will take a little time now to describe Mr Bernard, because he was such a striking figure it is

important for you to have an accurate mental image.)
Mr Bernard looked like an army drill sergeant. He
was six foot four, very muscly and his buzz cut hair
was so short you could see the veins on his head stick
out when he got angry (and they always stuck out
because he was always angry).

'Mr Bernard has only recently become a truancy
officer,' explained Headmaster Pimplestock, 'after
twenty-five years of being an army drill sergeant'
(which explained why he looked like a drill sergeant).

'Did you run away from the army?' asked Nanny
Piggins conversationally. 'I ran away from the circus.
I think it's good to branch out and embrace new
career opportunities.'

'Silence!' barked Mr Bernard. 'I have heard
all about you and your tricks and schemes. And I
will not have it. *Do-I-make-my-self-clear*?' (He had
a peculiar way of yelling each syllable individually
to emphasise his point.)

'Crystal clear,' said Nanny Piggins. 'I have both
perfect hearing and a comprehensive understanding
of English so there is no need to raise your voice
to me.'

'These three children will attend school every
day. *With-out-fail*,' barked Mr Bernard. 'I am not
some wishy-washy social worker. I have jumped out

of aeroplanes, swum swollen rivers, hiked across deserts and fought enemy agents with nothing but my bare hands. So if you keep these children out of school there is nothing you can do to stop me hunting them down and dragging them back here.'

'Oh really?' said Nanny Piggins as she narrowed her eyes and glared at the new truancy officer. The children all took a step back. They had seen that look before. Nanny Piggins did not like to be told she could not do something.

'Yes, really,' said Mr Bernard. 'Don't try to test me. I am way out of your league.'

'We'll see,' said Nanny Piggins.

'Yes, we will,' said Mr Bernard.

They both glared at each other for several minutes, neither wanting to be the first to look away.

'Um,' said Headmaster Pimplestock, 'I do have some paperwork to do. If I could have my office back?' (The problem with hiring the only truancy officer capable of intimidating Nanny Piggins was that he terrified Headmaster Pimplestock.)

'All right then,' said Mr Bernard, 'you're dismissed.'

'Thank you,' said Headmaster Pimplestock, who

actually started to leave the room himself before he realised that Mr Bernard was talking to Nanny Piggins.

Nanny Piggins turned to the children. 'Come along, let's go home.'

'No,' snapped Mr Bernard. 'It's one o'clock.'

'So?' asked Nanny Piggins.

'On a Tuesday. The children can't go home,' said Mr Bernard, his voice starting to rise again. 'They are supposed to be in class right now!'

'Oh, you want to start this new ridiculously strict regime today? All right, if you insist,' said Nanny Piggins. She turned to the children, 'I'll see you when you get home.' She then kissed each of them, picked up their frogs and left.

When the children got back from school they rushed to speak to their nanny. They found her in the kitchen working on her chocolate macaroon recipe.

'What are you going to do about the new truancy officer?' asked Derrick.

'Do? Oh nothing,' said Nanny Piggins, testing (eating) her seventy-ninth macaroon.

'Nothing?' asked Michael. He had fully expected

his nanny to have concocted a scheme to dangle Mr Bernard over a swimming pool full of raspberry jelly, or something equally exciting.

'I did think about punishing him for being rude,' admitted Nanny Piggins, 'but then I thought, it's his first day on a new job, he is probably feeling a little uncertain and a little out of his depth. So it would be much kinder of me to leave him alone for a few weeks while he settles in.'

'Leave him alone?!' Derrick was amazed.

'I don't take you out of school just to punish the truancy officer, you know,' said Nanny Piggins.

'Except that time you wanted to punish the truancy officer for ringing the doorbell in the middle of *The Young and the Irritable*,' Samantha reminded her.

'Oh yes, except for that one time, but she totally deserved it,' said Nanny Piggins.

The children nodded their agreement. It had been a particularly good episode in which Bethany had discovered that she was secretly her own twin sister.

'No, I think for a while, just to be kind to Mr Bernard, I will allow you to attend school the full four days a week,' announced Nanny Piggins.

'School is five days a week,' said Derrick.

'Really?!' said a shocked Nanny Piggins. 'That is an awful lot! Oh well, I suppose it won't hurt you to go for the full five days, for a week or two, if I make sure you have plenty of cake in your schoolbags.'

And so for three whole days Nanny Piggins allowed the Green children to attend school, provided they each took a huge suitcase full of treats with them, so they would not pass out from hunger or be forced to eat the rubbish (salad sandwiches) sold at the tuckshop.

But then, on the fourth day, something totally unexpected happened. The Green children genuinely got sick. Now the Green children normally got so much fresh air, sunshine and vitamin C (in the form of lemon cake) that they never got ill. So for them to actually catch a cold was very unusual. When the three of them woke up sneezing, coughing and running a fever Nanny Piggins insisted they stay in bed, eat lots of chocolate and watch lots of medicinal television.

'But what about Mr Bernard?' protested Michael. 'We'll all get in trouble.'

'Don't worry about that,' said Nanny Piggins.

'You are actually sick. I'm sure Mr Bernard will have the sense to see that you can't go down to a crowded school when you are packed full of dangerous virus cells ready to leap out of your bodies and attack the other children. I'll take care of it.'

Nanny Piggins went downstairs and rang the school. 'This is Nanny Piggins,' she said. 'I am ringing to inform you that Derrick, Samantha and Michael will not be attending school today because they have caught colds.'

'Really?' said the secretary on the other end of the line. She was quite disappointed. You see, there were three secretaries in the school office and when they saw the Green's home number come up on the caller ID, they always fought over who was going to take the call, because Nanny Piggins had such spectacularly entertaining excuses.

Since she had become the Green's nanny, Nanny Piggins had rung up the school saying that the children had smallpox, bigpox, cowpox, Mad Cow's Disease, Bubonic Plague, ESP, athlete's foot, athlete's leg, athlete's dishpan hands, malaria, diphtheria, foot and mouth disease, rickets and temporary blindness due to low blood chocolate levels. So as you can imagine, the secretary was disappointed to hear that the children had contracted something as mundane as a cold. 'Oh, I'm sorry to hear that. I'll make a note of it.'

Nanny Piggins had barely placed the telephone back in its cradle before it rang. She picked it up.

'Hello,' said Nanny Piggins.

'I have just been informed of your intentions to blatantly disregard my directive,' barked Mr Bernard.

'If you mean that the children have colds, then yes, they have colds,' said Nanny Piggins. She did not really want to have a protracted conversation with Mr Bernard. The children were running fevers, so she wanted to get back upstairs and tend to them with some cooling chocolate ice-cream.

'You're lying!' accused Mr Bernard.

Nanny Piggins gasped. This was no way to speak to a lady. 'Would you like me to get a doctor to come and confirm my diagnosis?' she asked.

'Ha!' said Mr Bernard. 'I have no trouble believing that you have some doctor in your pocket ready to back up your duplicitous schemes.' (As it happens Nanny Piggins did have a doctor friend who would do almost anything for her, ever since she had agreed to stop ruining his practice with her holistic cake-healing business.) 'No, I don't believe it for a moment,' continued Mr Bernard. 'I am coming to collect the children. I will be there in thirty minutes.' With which he slammed down the telephone.

'Well I never,' said Nanny Piggins to herself. She was at a loss. That was the problem with arguing with someone over the telephone, she could not end the conversation the way she wanted to because you could not bite someone's leg via a phone line.

'Is everything all right, Nanny Piggins?' asked Samantha. She had struggled out of bed and come to investigate when she heard the phone ring. Nanny Piggins looked up at her. Samantha was white and sweaty and she had her worried face on. There was no way Nanny Piggins was going to let some big bullying truancy officer manhandle this poor sick girl.

'Everything is absolutely fine,' said Nanny Piggins. 'Mr Bernard will be popping down for a quick chat. But that won't be a problem at all. I'm going to get Boris to come and sit with you and tell you Russian folktales while I pop out to get a few things. We must make our visitor welcome.'

So while Boris took care of the children, Nanny Piggins went out to fetch supplies. But she did not go to the bakery to buy a cake as she normally would for a visitor. Nanny Piggins deemed Mr Bernard to be unworthy of bakery cake. Instead, she went to the building site at the end of the block and asked the builders if she could borrow their bulldozer. Naturally they agreed – they all loved Nanny Piggins because she made them flapjacks and put on trapeze shows by swinging from their demolition ball.

When Mr Bernard arrived, precisely thirty minutes after he had issued his threat, he was astonished to discover that the Green's ordinary suburban house was surrounded by a two-and-a-half-metre-wide moat on all four sides. And Nanny Piggins was leaning out the living-room window as she finished filling up the moat with water from a garden hose. When Nanny Piggins saw Mr Bernard she called out to him, 'Hello, Mr Bernard, sorry you can't see the children, they're infectious.' Then she slammed the window shut.

Mr Bernard was bewildered. But he had never let a little thing like emotions slow him down in wartime and he was determined to apply the same principals here.

Mr Bernard went to knock on the front door, then realised he could not. For a start, to do so he would have to cross the moat. And secondly, the front door had been entirely covered up by a raised drawbridge (which Nanny Piggins had made herself using the heavy 200-year-old door from the town hall. Technically she had not asked permission before she borrowed it, but none of the public servants going in or out of the building had had the courage to stop her).

For the first time, the thought crossed Mr Bernard's mind that perhaps he had underestimated this pig. Mr Bernard had heard that Nanny Piggins was tricky, yet he had not expected her to construct a medieval fortress in under thirty minutes. But he soon dismissed this idea as irrelevant. He had chased arms' smugglers through the jungles of Sri Lanka, tracked rebels through snowstorms in Afghanistan and been the army's hand-to-hand combat champion three times in a row. He was sure he could handle one petite pig.

Mr Bernard turned his attention to the moat. 'It's going to take more than a puddle to stop me!' he yelled at the house.

'Sorry, I can't hear you, I'm too busy looking after sick children,' lied Nanny Piggins (her ears were perfectly capable of multi-tasking).

Nanny Piggins, Boris and the sick children were really all peering through the upstairs window. They did not want to miss what would happen next.

Mr Bernard put his foot forward and stepped

into the moat. This was his first mistake. He had assumed, given the little time she'd had, that Nanny Piggins would have dug a shallow moat that he could wade across. But Nanny Piggins did not do things by half measures. Indeed, there was no need to do so when you had borrowed a giant bulldozer. The moat she had dug was three metres deep, as Mr Bernard discovered when he plunged into the icy cold water all the way up to his buzz cut.

'Agh!' he cried involuntarily. Because even battle-hardened soldiers hate being plunged into cold water. He then struggled to scramble out, which was a lot harder than he expected because Nanny Piggins had made the lawn extra specially slippery by smearing gallons and gallons of raspberry jelly on it (while she had decided not to dangle Mr Bernard over a swimming pool full of raspberry jelly, she had prepared the jelly just in case).

So by the time Mr Bernard scrambled up on the grass, he was soaking wet, sticky with jelly and panting to catch his breath. He scanned the house, deciding where he was going to attempt to infiltrate next.

Nanny Piggins pushed open the upstairs window and called down to him, 'Would you like a towel?'

Mr Bernard shook his fist at her. 'I'm coming to take those children to school!'

'It really would be better if you gave up now,' urged Nanny Piggins. 'I'd hate to see you injure yourself.'

Mr Bernard did not respond. Instead he went to his van to fetch some equipment.

When he first got this job he had visited the former truancy officer in the recuperation home and she had advised him on the hardware he would need. At the time he had thought that the extensive list of tradesman's tools she recommended was a product of her traumatised mind, but now he realised that it was excellent advice from a sensible woman. Thankfully he had listened to her, so Mr Bernard had just what he needed on hand. He slid a military surplus inflatable dinghy out of his van, along with a set of bolt cutters and an angle grinder.

Mr Bernard pulled the ripcord on the dinghy so that it inflated immediately and he set it on the moat water. Then he picked up his angle grinder and bolt cutters and started paddling towards the drawbridge. He was just standing up in the dingy (never a particularly stable thing to do) and reaching up to the chains that held the drawbridge in place, about to cut them off with his angle grinder, when suddenly he was hit in the head by a barrage of rock cakes.

Now, naturally, you will be horrified. It is so uncharacteristic of Nanny Piggins to waste her own delicious rock cakes on assaulting something as unworthy as a truancy officer's head. But rest assured, they were not her own rock cakes. Nanny Piggins' rock cakes were light, fluffy and delicious and, therefore, totally unsuitable for attacking would-be home intruders. So Nanny Piggins had nipped down to Nanny Anne's house and borrowed four dozen of her rock cakes, which were full of pureed beetroot and grated carrot, and therefore as hard as actual rocks (and much less tasty).

As a result, Mr Bernard started to wobble and nothing is more wobbly than a big man in a small dinghy. He was soon toppling back into the freezing water and dropping his angle grinder to the murky depths, never to be seen again.

It is at this point that the Police Sergeant arrived, as Mr Bernard splashed about in the moat hurling abuse at Nanny Piggins, and as Nanny Piggins, Boris and the children leaned out of the window, smiling. Even the children were starting to look better. It is amazing the recuperative effect of seeing a big bully make a fool of himself.

'What have we here?' asked the Police Sergeant, standing over Mr Bernard in the moat.

'Arrest that pig!' demanded Mr Bernard. 'She is wilfully keeping those children out of school. And she has assaulted me repeatedly.'

'Really? We have had several complaints from the neighbours,' said the Police Sergeant, taking out his notebook.

'Did you hear that, Piggins, you're in for it now,' called Mr Bernard.

'The complaints have not been about Nanny Piggins,' corrected the Police Sergeant. 'I think you'll find that on this street she is a respected member of the community.' Which was true.

While Nanny Piggins did sometimes steal mail, break into other peoples' houses in search of cake ingredients and leap into other peoples' gardens as part of her inexplicably dramatic children's games, she also made sure there were absolutely no burglaries on the street, no loitering teenagers, and no door-to-door salesmen (her reputation for leg biting was so widespread). She baked everyone on the street a cake for their birthdays, anniversaries, christenings, weddings, funerals and bar mitzvahs (on the condition they shared several pieces with her). And while the neighbours rolled their eyes and despaired of her behaviour at times, she was also beloved. So when the people in the street looked out their windows and saw a great big man yelling at Nanny Piggins and trying to break into her house, they naturally called the police.

'What?' blustered Mr Bernard. Having been an army drill sergeant for twenty-five years, he was unused to situations that did not involve him being the bully and everyone else having to put up with it.

'We have had several reports of a large angry-looking man with an unfortunate haircut yelling threats at this diminutive pig and the three children in her care,' read the Police Sergeant from his notes. 'Also that you have used power tools in your attempts to break into her home.'

'But I'm the truancy officer,' spluttered Mr Bernard.

'That does not give you the right to trespass or vandalise private property,' chided the Police Sergeant.

'She started it,' whined Mr Bernard. Like all bullies, he fell apart when someone who was not bobbing about in a moat stood over him and told him off.

'I'm afraid I'm going to have to arrest you for being a public nuisance,' said the Police Sergeant.

'We are going to be in so much trouble on Monday,' said Derrick, as he watched the truancy officer get dragged away by the police.

'Oh I don't think you'll ever see him again,' said Nanny Piggins.

'Really, why not?' asked Samantha.

'Well, after he's dried off and washed the jelly out of his clothes, I suspect he will look back on this whole incident and decide he's much better off going back to the military,' predicted Nanny Piggins.

And she was entirely right. By the end of the day the truancy officer could not wait to get back to the army, because he felt much safer in a war zone than in Nanny Piggins' front yard.

The next day Headmaster Pimplestock summoned Nanny Piggins back to his office. 'You do realise that by driving off Mr Bernard I will have to re-hire Miss Britches,' complained Headmaster Pimplestock.

'I think it's for the best,' said Nanny Piggins. 'True, she did follow us and peer in our windows at the most inconvenient times. But on the whole we got along with her very well.'

'She never caught you. Not once,' said the headmaster.

'Exactly,' agreed Nanny Piggins.

CHAPTER 3

Nanny Piggins and the Accidental Blast-off

'Yeeeeeehiyyaaaahhh!' bellowed Nanny Piggins as she fired a rubber dart at a clump of bushes.

'Take that!' screamed Michael, flinging a water bomb at the same hapless plants.

'And that!' yelled Samantha, letting fly with Samson Wallace's salad sandwich.

'Hold the defensive position!' ordered Nanny Piggins. 'Don't let them surround us! Victory will soon be ours!'

Nanny Piggins, Boris and the children were having a lovely time at the park fighting for the land rights of Native Americans. They did this every Saturday morning. It had started out as a game of cowboys and Indians, but then Nanny Piggins read up on the history of early American settlement and nobody wanted to be cowboys anymore. The Indians were much more fun. They wore striking costumes that involved face paint and feathers, and they had vengeance on their side (Nanny Piggins loved fighting for vengeance).

So every weekend they would gather with the other neighbourhood children, then lay siege to the playground equipment and fight off the cowboys. It worked out to be a surprisingly pacifistic game, because all the enemies were imaginary, so there were very few injuries, unless you counted the plants. (The grass had been scalped so many times it no longer needed mowing.)

On this particular morning their mission was to protect The Lost Treasure of Brown Gold (a large supply of chocolate Nanny Piggins had brought along for their mid-morning snack) from the rampaging attack of General Cowardy Custard (who was, for the purposes of the exercise, being played by a particularly savage-looking begonia bush).

As such, they were so engrossed in their military planning that they did not notice when three black SUVs pulled up and a team of men in grey suits got out. If Nanny Piggins *had* noticed them she certainly would have found them intriguing, because they seemed to be talking to each other via their sleeve cuffs, usually something only super-spies in movies did.

When one of the men stepped forward and yelled into a bullhorn, 'Sarah Matahari Lorelai Piggins, come out and give yourself up!' Nanny Piggins assumed it was just one of the parents getting involved in the fun. So naturally she threw a bucket of dirt at him and said, 'If you take one step nearer I'll scalp you!'

The men were not sure what to do. They had been trained to take threats of terrorism seriously, but it was hard to take them seriously when they came from a petite pig wearing a lovely pink dress and matching bolero jacket. However, like Nanny Piggins, they enjoyed a little bit of violence, so on balance they decided to charge the play equipment, much to the delight of the children who had a wonderful time keeping them at bay by throwing water balloons and fending them off with sticks. (Nanny Piggins had taught the children the ancient art of Kendo only the previous weekend, so they were all very handy with a stick.)

After half an hour of struggle the men eventually retreated to the safety of the park's gazebo, to treat their wounds and revise their strategy. This gave Nanny Piggins and the children a wonderful opportunity to hide The Lost Treasure of Brown Gold – in their stomachs.

The men in the gazebo had a long and animated discussion (with much finger pointing and some weeping), then one of them went back to his SUV, opened the door and pulled out a timid-looking man wearing wire-rimmed glasses and a white lab coat. The suited man handed him the bullhorn and marched him over to the play equipment.

'Er, um, Sarah Piggins?' said the timid man into the bullhorn.

'Are you ready to surrender?' demanded Nanny Piggins.

'No, um, I think there's been a little misunderstanding,' said the timid man. 'We're not here to play.'

'Well then, you're a fool,' said Nanny Piggins, 'because we're having a jolly good game.'

'It's me, Peter, from the circus,' said the timid man.

'Peter?' said Nanny Piggins, whipping out her binoculars for a closer look. 'My cannon assistant! How wonderful to see you. Who do you fire out of cannons these days?'

'I don't do that anymore,' admitted Peter. 'I got a proper job.'

'Oh no!' exclaimed Nanny Piggins. 'What a shame! You had such a talent for gunpowder.'

'I got a job at NASA,' explained Peter.

'The Naughty Association for Sneaky Acrobats?' asked Nanny Piggins.

'No,' said Peter.

'Good,' said Nanny Piggins. 'You don't want to fall in with them. They never pick up their share of a restaurant bill.'

'I work on the space program,' continued Peter. 'I help launch the space shuttle. At least I would if I could. For some reason we can't get it to take-off. We've tried everything – recalibrating the computers, dismantling the engines, rewiring the electrical system . . .'

'Did you try kicking it and pressing the "go" button lots of times?' asked Nanny Piggins.

'Yes, that too,' said Peter. 'The greatest aeronautical engineers in the world have been working on it, but with no luck. That's why I'm here. I told my boss, "No-one knows more about being blasted than Sarah Piggins, the world's greatest flying pig.'"

'It's true,' agreed Nanny Piggins.

'We're supposed to be launching the space shuttle this Saturday,' explained Peter, 'but we're going to look pretty silly, with the whole world's media watching, if we can't even turn the engines on.'

'So you want me to come and put on a tap dancing show to distract them?' guessed Nanny Piggins.

'No,' said Peter. 'We were wondering if you could help us fix the space shuttle?'

'Of course! Why didn't you say so?' said Nanny Piggins. 'I'll just have to pop home and pack some cake.'

'No need,' said Peter. 'When I knew we were going to try to recruit you, I took the liberty of hiring a team of pastry chefs to be on stand-by at all times.'

'This is why you were such a great assistant,' praised Nanny Piggins.

And so Nanny Piggins, Boris and the children were flown out to Houston to see if they could rescue the space program. But when they arrived at NASA they were not given the welcome they'd been expecting.

'When you said you knew a flying pig who might be able to help,' yelled the head of NASA, 'I thought you were talking metaphorically!'

'Oh no,' said Nanny Piggins. 'When they say I am a flying pig, they mean I am a flying pig. I won't stand for false advertising.'

'We can't let a pig into the space shuttle!' raged the head of NASA. 'It is a scientifically controlled environment.'

'It's all right, I am prepared for the worst,' said Nanny Piggins. 'I know astronauts have terrible body odour. But I have a strong will, so I will tolerate it.'

'What choice do we have, sir?' reasoned Peter. 'Nobody else has been able to fix the problem.'

The head of NASA considered this. They had tried everything short of turning to circus animals, and he was desperate. 'All right, but let's assemble a topnotch team of experts to work with her, so they can watch her like a hawk.'

'No need,' said Nanny Piggins. 'I've brought my own team.'

'Where?' asked the head of NASA, trying to look around Boris and the children to see if there were any top scientists behind them that he had not noticed.

'Derrick is in charge of supplies,' explained Nanny Piggins (which, to her mind, meant cake), 'Samantha is in charge of taking down notes,' continued Nanny Piggins (which, to her mind, meant taking down orders for cake), 'and Michael is second-in-command for both supplies and taking down notes – he's very versatile.'

'And I suppose next you'll be telling me your bear is of vital scientific importance,' said the head of NASA sarcastically.

'Oh yes, he is the morale officer,' said Nanny Piggins. 'If we can't work out your problem right away, he will be in charge of cheering us all up by doing a little ballet.'

'This is ridiculous – I am not letting a pig, three children and a dancing bear get into the space shuttle – it is a multi-billion dollar piece of space exploration technology.'

'If you don't let me fix it for you,' said Nanny Piggins, 'it's a multi-billion dollar paperweight.'

'She's right, sir,' agreed Peter. 'What have you got to lose?'

'My dignity, my respected place in the scientific community, my position as head of NASA,' said the head of NASA.

'Pish!' said Nanny Piggins. 'Who cares about

silly things like that? Now, has anyone got a crowbar and a wrench they can lend me so I can sort this problem out? I'd like to get on with it so I can get home in time to see *The Young and the Irritable*.'

And so the head of NASA went to sulk in his office, while Nanny Piggins, Boris and the children were led away to the space shuttle. They had to put on orange jumpsuits before they were allowed inside, which delighted Nanny Piggins.

'What a brilliant idea to wear a jumpsuit over your clothes,' she enthused. 'Now if any of my chocolate falls out of my pockets, it will gather around the elasticated ankles and not be lost.'

Nanny Piggins was not permitted to take a crowbar or wrench onboard. The technicians insisted that the equipment was too delicate. Instead they gave her a tiny allen key, a tiny screwdriver and a tiny flashlight. Then she was given strict instructions not to use any of them without writing a full report both before and after, detailing exactly what she had done.

As they drove across the runway towards the space shuttle, they could see it was much bigger than it looked on television, and much more peculiar looking. It was kind of like a squat stubby aeroplane that someone had accidentally parked pointing directly upwards at the sky.

When they arrived at the launch site, Nanny Piggins, Boris and the children rode a lift up to the nose of the shuttle.

'Are you sure this is safe?' worried Samantha.

'It's fine,' said Nanny Piggins. 'We catch lifts all the time in department stores.'

'Not the lift,' said Samantha, 'I mean the space shuttle.'

'I'd worry more about the lift,' said Nanny Piggins. 'But then I have always had a dread fear of being caught in a confined space with insufficient cake supplies.'

'We forgot to leave a note for Father saying we wouldn't be home for dinner,' said Michael.

'What is he going to think if we are in a terrible space shuttle accident?' panicked Samantha.

'That he will have to get his own dinner, I suppose,' said Nanny Piggins, 'which, no doubt, he'll find upsetting. But I'm sure he'll struggle through.'

'Don't worry,' said Boris, giving the children a reassuring hug. 'Nanny Piggins knows what she's doing.'

'But she doesn't know anything about computers, space shuttles or space travel,' said Derrick.

'Yes, but if anyone can pick it up in five minutes, Nanny Piggins can,' said Boris confidently.

'Difficult things are almost never as difficult as they seem,' explained Nanny Piggins, 'except for sudoku. They're impossible.'

Entering the cabin was tricky, because the space shuttle was pointing up and all the chairs were lying back. So getting about inside was more like climbing around a jungle gym than walking about inside an aeroplane.

The hardest thing was getting Boris in through the doorway. Apparently the space shuttle door had not been designed with a 700 kilogram bear in mind. Fortunately Boris happened to have a seven litre bucket of honey with him, which they were able to smear around the doorframe as lubricant. So, eventually, with the children and Nanny Piggins pulling on the inside, and the NASA ground crew pushing from the outside, he was able to get inside with one big 'POP'.

'What do we do first?' asked Derrick.

'Let's see,' said Nanny Piggins thoughtfully. She looked about. Then she sniffed about. Then she licked her trotter and held it in the air. The children were completely silent while she concentrated.

'There!' declared Nanny Piggins, pointing dramatically at one small panel in the wall. 'There is something wrong with the wiring behind that panel.'

'There is?' said Derrick, astounded.

Nanny Piggins clambered across the shuttle and used her allen key to access the panel (without writing a full report beforehand).

'Aha, just as I suspected,' announced Nanny Piggins. 'These two wires are crossed!'

'How do you know?' asked Samantha in amazement.

'There was a faint aroma of quadruple espresso coffee, parmesan cheese and poorly made burritos coming from this vicinity,' explained Nanny Piggins, 'which tells me that someone, who was overtired after a night of being sick from eating bad Mexican food, was working on this panel. And as soon as I opened it I could see it was all wrong.'

'You could?' marvelled Michael, as he looked at the web of hundreds of different coloured wires woven in every direction.

'Oh yes,' said Nanny Piggins. 'As you can see, this blue wire leads to this green wire. And everyone knows those two colours clash.'

'Blue and green should never been seen,' quoted Boris solemnly.

'Exactly,' said Nanny Piggins. 'And over here, there is a red wire leading to a pink wire! Yuck! I can barely look at it, it's so unsightly.'

'It is?' asked Michael.

'That poor engineer,' sympathised Boris. 'He must have been so exhausted not to realise he was making such a dreadful colour mistake.'

'I'll swap them back,' said Nanny Piggins, whipping out a pair of wire cutters she just happened to have hidden in her hairdo.

'But you can't just start cutting wires on the space shuttle!' exclaimed Derrick.

'Why not?' asked Nanny Piggins. 'I can't leave something as ugly as this. It's like walking past a crooked picture and not straightening it. Or not throwing a blanket over your father's face when he's fallen asleep on the sofa.' Nanny Piggins deftly snipped the wires and crossed the colours over. 'You see – blue and red, and green and pink – much nicer.'

'Please don't snip any more wires,' begged Samantha.

'Of course not,' agreed Nanny Piggins as she shut the panel door. 'Now we'll just turn her on to see if that's fixed it.'

'When you say "turn her on", you don't mean

the whole space shuttle, do you?' asked Michael, beginning to panic as much as his sister. If his nanny did manage to destroy the space shuttle he imagined they would get into even more trouble than the time she 'accidentally' ran over Headmaster Pimplestock's bicycle with a steamroller.

'Don't worry, it'll be fine,' said Nanny Piggins as she clambered over to the main controls. 'I hope it's like a car and the radio will come on when you turn the engine on . . . Hmm, there's no key to turn . . . But this big green button looks promising; I'll try that.'

Nothing happened.

'Maybe I pressed the wrong button,' said Nanny Piggins. 'I'll try a few more.' She swiftly tapped her trotter on every button, flicked every switch and pushed every slider within arm's reach (which was a lot because there are a lot of buttons and switches within arm's reach of the pilot's seat in a space shuttle).

Again, nothing happened.

'I knew I should have brought a crowbar,' muttered Nanny Piggins.

But then, suddenly, the space shuttle shuddered, red lights started flashing and an automated voice boomed out of the speakers: 'Commencing launch procedures in ten . . .'

'It worked!' cried Nanny Piggins delightedly.

'Nine . . .' said the automated voice.

'It worked!' screamed the children in horror.

'Don't panic,' said Nanny Piggins. 'I'll just switch it off again. Now, what did I press?'

'Eight . . .' said the automated voice.

'You don't remember?!' shrieked Samantha over the roar of the engines that had just fired up.

'Seven . . .' said the automated voice.

'Perhaps we'd better sit in the seats and put our safety belts on, just in case,' suggested Boris.

'Six . . .' said the automated voice.

'Good thinking,' agreed Nanny Piggins. 'Safety belts are so important, as anyone who has ever read about Newtonian physics knows.'

'Five . . .' said the automated voice.

'You are still trying to stop the launch, aren't you?' asked Michael.

'Four . . .' said the automated voice.

'Oh yes, of course,' said Nanny Piggins. 'I know, I'll just bang the green button again lots of times and see if that helps.'

'Three . . .' said the automated voice.

Nanny Piggins pressed buttons furiously but the engines still roared and the space shuttle still shuddered.

'I don't know why they have to make it all so complicated,' muttered Nanny Piggins. 'We don't have any buttons on cannons and they still manage to fire people all right.'

'Two . . .' said the automated voice.

'This is ground control. What the heck do you think you are doing?! Turn that space shuttle off immediately!' screamed the head of NASA.

'All right, no need to yell,' chided Nanny Piggins, 'although perhaps you can tell me which button exactly should I be pressing?'

'One . . .' said the automated voice.

'The big red one!' screamed the head of NASA.

But Nanny Piggins never got to press the big red button because just as she reached forward, the space shuttle launched, and the force of it accelerating at 4793 kilometres per hour pushed her back in her seat.

'We're going to die!' wailed Samantha. She would have fainted but there is no way you can collapse when 3Gs of force are holding you in a sitting position.

'This is so cool!' yelled Michael.

'Samson Wallace is going to be totally jealous,' agreed Derrick.

The shuttle burst through the atmosphere and

out into space. The shuddering stopped, the engines turned off and everything went silent. The five of them did not say anything for a moment because there was so much adrenaline pumping through their systems.

'Well, I got it going all right, didn't I?' said Nanny Piggins proudly.

'Well done, Sarah,' said Boris.

'Hey, look out the window!' exclaimed Michael.

(Now reader, I am sure you know that little children generally do not enjoy looking at views. The idea of going on a long car journey and being told to look out the window is, to most children, akin to the very worst kind of torture. But in this instance, Derrick, Samantha and Michael looked out the window and were struck speechless by the beauty of what they saw. The vast infinity of space was utterly black, but this darkness was lit up like a Christmas tree by a million stars spread out in every direction. And the stars twinkled, really twinkled, and so much brighter than they did down on Earth, where you can only see them through all the gases of the atmosphere.)

'Look at that!' exclaimed Derrick, as the space shuttle tilted, adjusting its course and the Earth came into view beneath them. They saw the bright blues of the ocean, the greens and browns of the continents and the white of the clouds, all contained in a perfect sphere and highlighted against the deep unending blackness of space. It was awesome.

'Well,' said Nanny Piggins as their brains finally began to process the extraordinary situation they had found themselves in. 'I think whatever trouble we will get in when we land will be totally worth it.'

And even Samantha, who would easily win the gold medal if worrying was an Olympic sport, nodded her head in agreement.

'So,' said Nanny Piggins, 'now that we're up here, what are we going to do?'

The children turned to look at her. They were even more agog at their nanny than they were at the view. 'You're not planning to take the space shuttle anywhere, are you?' asked Derrick, suspecting his nanny of harbouring ideas of a quick visit to Mars.

'Oh no, of course not,' said Nanny Piggins, looking wistfully at the red dot seventy-eight million kilometres away. 'That would be naughty. We don't want to get in too much trouble. I imagine we'll just orbit Earth a couple of times and then land, once they've sorted themselves out down at ground control.'

It was a relief to hear their nanny sounding so sensible.

'But that will probably take a couple of hours,' added Nanny Piggins, 'so how are we going to amuse ourselves in the meantime?'

'Hmmm,' said Boris thoughtfully. 'Perhaps we should have a snack?'

'Brilliant suggestion,' agreed Nanny Piggins.

But when they took off their seatbelts to go in search of food they discovered something even more wonderful than the view out the window. They discovered they were weightless. And in the absence of gravity even Boris was able to float around like a butterfly. It was an amazing sensation. The children tumbled through the air, spun in pirouettes and hung upside down with their heads off the floor. They felt like the greatest acrobats on Earth, except that they were not on Earth anymore, so they could not really claim the title. And when Boris tried out some of his ballet moves they were even more beautiful, poetic and graceful than they were back home.

Eventually, after an hour of play, Nanny Piggins remembered that they were all hungry so they resumed their search for snacks. They soon found the food storage closet at the back of the ship. But when they opened it, they experienced their first disappointment in space travel.

'Where is all the cake?' asked a bewildered Nanny Piggins as she rifled through endless sachets. 'I can't find anything. No biscuits, no tarts, no doughnuts, no cheesecake . . . How are astronauts meant to survive up here?'

'I think these sachets are food,' said Derrick.

'No!' exclaimed Nanny Piggins in shock. 'Surely not.'

'Now, Sarah, you should be open-minded,' said Boris. 'Remember, just because food looks disgusting doesn't mean it is.'

'It's usually a good warning sign,' muttered Nanny Piggins.

'I'll try one,' volunteered Michael.

'You're a brave, brave boy,' praised Nanny Piggins.

Michael took a sachet, tore it open and squeezed it into his mouth. The others did not need to ask if it tasted good. They could tell from Michael's expression. His face went red, his mouth puckered up and his eyes started to water. He would have spat it back out again, but he was worried where the spit would go in zero gravity.

'That was awful!' exclaimed Michael, after finally summoning the courage to swallow.

Samantha read the label: 'Liver with brussels sprouts.'

'How unspeakably dreadful!' said a horrified Nanny Piggins. 'No wonder NASA needed me. If they haven't got the brains to keep a nice chocolate cake on board for the astronauts, it's no surprise they can't build a working space shuttle.'

Just then the speakers crackled and the head of NASA's voice boomed through the cockpit. (I will not print exactly what he said because he used a lot of rude words, which were unbecoming of a man of science, and really, it is ungentlemanly to yell at a lady.) After a full five minutes of recriminations and tellings-off (him telling Nanny Piggins off for launching the space shuttle and her telling him off for using naughty words in front of children), he eventually calmed down.

'All right,' said the head of NASA. 'At 1500 hours we will need you to commence landing procedure.'

'What did he say?' asked Nanny Piggins. 'He's not speaking Latin, is he? I absolutely refuse to be spoken to in Latin. It's a language entirely for show-offs.'

'He said at three o'clock he wants you to start the landing,' explained Derrick.

'Ohhh,' said Nanny Piggins. 'He likes using his fifty-cent words, doesn't he?'

'I can hear every word you are saying!' yelled the head of NASA. He was beginning to lose his temper again.

'I know,' said Nanny Piggins, 'but unlike some people, I don't say things I should be ashamed of.' (If she could have seen the head of NASA at that moment, she would have seen him blush.)

'Because this was an unplanned launch our computers are not properly in sync with the shuttle,' explained the head of NASA, 'so you will need to get out the workbook from the aft locker, copy in the readouts from the cockpit displays, use the coordinates I give you, and calculate your re-entry angle using trigonometry.'

'Oh,' said Nanny Piggins, and for the first time that day she began to feel genuinely sorry that she had become the first pig in space. Because there was nothing in the world that she hated more than doing maths. Nanny Piggins was, however, a brave pig so she got out the workbook, copied down the readouts and gave it a valiant effort. She attempted to do trigonometry for an entire twenty seconds before she got heartily sick of it, cried, 'Piffle to that!' and flushed the whole workbook down the space toilet.

'But how are we going to land now?!' worried Samantha.

'Don't worry,' Nanny Piggins reassured her. 'I was blasted out of a cannon night after night for years. I know more about landings than all that lot down at NASA put together. I'll just land it by eye.'

'But we have to re-enter Earth's atmosphere at exactly the right angle or we'll burn up!' exclaimed Derrick.

'I don't believe that for a second,' dismissed Nanny Piggins. 'I think that's just a load of old tosh they made up to make space travel movies more exciting. I'm sure we'll be fine. I never burnt up on re-entry when I smashed out through the Big Top and had to smash my way back in.'

'But this is rather different . . .' protested Michael.

'Now, children,' chided Boris. 'Nanny Piggins has made a decision. She almost always knows what she is doing, or is very good at faking it, so let's stop being Nelly-negatives and start being supportive.'

'All I need is something to aim at down on the ground,' said Nanny Piggins, peering out through the windscreen of the shuttle as Earth passed beneath them.

'You could land it in the ocean,' said Derrick as they passed over the Pacific.

'Good gracious no!' exclaimed Nanny Piggins.

'I've got a lovely new pair of suede boots on and I don't want to get them wet.'

'How about the Sahara desert?' suggested Michael. He had just read a thrilling book about searching for diamonds in the Sahara.

'Too much sand,' dismissed Boris. 'It would take forever to brush out of my fur.'

'I know,' exclaimed Nanny Piggins. 'Look down there – it's the Great Wall of China. We'll aim for that.'

The others peered out the window to see a thin line winding its way across China.

'Do you think you can hit it?' asked Derrick.

'Easily,' said Nanny Piggins. 'The Great Wall of China is over a thousand miles long, so I'm sure I can hit some part of it.'

'But won't the Chinese get cross?' protested Samantha.

'I don't see why they would,' said Nanny Piggins. 'They don't use it to keep out the rampaging Mongol hordes anymore so it's just sitting there doing nothing.'

Nanny Piggins took the controls of the space shuttle and started pressing the buttons that she thought would make it land.

The speakers crackled. 'What are you doing?'

yelled the head of NASA. 'Why are you pressing buttons? Have you done your trigonometry?'

'Keep your hair on,' said Nanny Piggins. 'I'm just bringing her in to land.'

'But—but you don't know how!' spluttered the head of NASA.

'That didn't stop me launching it, did it?' Nanny Piggins reminded him.

'That is a multi-billion dollar piece of machinery,' the head of NASA wailed.

'And I'm about to return it to you,' said Nanny Piggins. 'Really, this fellow needs to make up his mind what he wants. Now stop talking to me while I'm trying to pilot the space shuttle.' Nanny Piggins turned off the speakers (she had figured out where that switch was). 'Strap yourselves in. I'm taking her down.' Nanny Piggins turned the nose of the space shuttle in towards the atmosphere, gave the engines a blast and before they knew it they were rocketing back towards Earth.

The space shuttle shuddered, the atmosphere seared the outside of the windscreen, and the wind whistled against the wings. The g-force once again pinned Boris and the children to their seats.

'Is everything all right, Nanny Piggins?' asked Derrick.

'Tickety-boo!' Nanny Piggins assured him.

After several unpleasant seconds of being shaken about like an old shoe in a washing machine that was inexplicably being blasted by a blowtorch, they finally broke through the upper atmosphere.

'You see!' cried Nanny Piggins. 'I told you we wouldn't burn up.'

Having not exploded, the children now began to worry about not crashing. They could see China rapidly approaching as the space shuttle part-glided and part-dropped like a stone towards it.

'Now where is that wall?' muttered Nanny Piggins. 'I could have sworn it was here somewhere.'

'Oh no,' moaned Samantha.

'It's all right,' said Nanny Piggins. 'I've spotted it! It's up ahead.'

Suddenly the famous icon of fourteenth century Chinese architecture appeared among the trees in front of them.

'And there's a nice flat spot,' exclaimed Nanny Piggins. 'This is working out well. I'll just put her down.'

Nanny Piggins lowered the landing gear, put up the flaps, lifted the nose and with a big – BANG! – made contact with the Great Wall of China. The shuttle shook and the brakes screeched, leaving two long strips of rubber along the top of the wall. Then, eventually, after what felt like a lifetime of shrieking brakes and grinding metal, they came to a complete halt. If it had been on a runway, and not on a tourist attraction in a foreign country, it would have been a perfect textbook landing.

'Easy-peasy,' said Nanny Piggins. 'I don't see why people make such a fuss about astronauts. Flying a space shuttle is nowhere near as hard as making caramel baskets from scratch. Shall we get out and see if we can find a Chinese restaurant nearby? I'm starving.'

As it turned out, they did not need to find a restaurant because the President of China personally invited them to a banquet at the People's Palace. After all, no pig had ever landed a space shuttle on the Great Wall of China before and he thought it was important to mark the occasion. Then, as soon as the meal was over, the President had armed guards escort them to the border, where they were made to promise never to return to China, except via an aeroplane and carrying passports.

When they got back to Houston, the head of NASA was less kind about the whole thing. He yelled at Nanny Piggins using words so rude she had to go home and look several of them up in a dictionary. But despite his threats and accusations, the head of NASA did not have her arrested or sent to prison, because he so desperately wanted the whole affair hushed up. He was not sure what he wanted the media to know less. That he had allowed a pig, a bear and three children into the space shuttle . . . or that he had been unable to stop the space shuttle landing on the Great Wall of China . . . or that he had been cutting costs by giving the astronauts nothing but liver and brussels sprouts to eat (which was the first thing Nanny Piggins threatened to reveal if she sold her story).

The head of NASA even gave Peter, Nanny Piggins' old cannon assistant, a promotion. Because whatever else had happened, no-one could deny it had been his suggestion of hiring a flying pig that got the space shuttle going again. Which just goes to show why lateral thinking is so important.

And so Nanny Piggins, Boris and the children returned home having only been away for two nights. Mr Green had not even noticed that they were gone. He just grumbled that there had been nothing in the fridge for his dinner except six chocolate mud cakes. Fortunately he had only eaten half of one, so there was a lovely snack waiting for the weary space travellers.

'Are you glad you finally got to try space travel?' asked Michael.

'Oh yes, I've been meaning to give it a go for years,' said Nanny Piggins. 'But, on the whole, I'd much rather be right here in this kitchen eating cake than orbiting Earth and eating brussels sprouts. Some sacrifices are just too much.' The children agreed heartily as they ate their seventh helpings of chocolate cake. Because no-one ever had seventh helpings of brussels sprouts.

CHAPTER 4

Nanny Piggins and the Giant Lollipop

When Derrick, Samantha and Michael got off their school bus, they were surprised to see Boris standing there waiting for them.

'Where's Nanny Piggins?' asked Derrick.

'I don't know,' admitted Boris. 'She burst into my shed, announced that she had a very important meeting to go to and then ran off.'

'Oh dear,' said Samantha. 'That doesn't sound good.'

'Was she happy-excited or worried-excited?' asked Michael.

'It doesn't make much difference, does it?' asked Derrick. 'Either way she always seems to end up in the same amount of trouble.'

Just then the children got to see exactly what sort of excited Nanny Piggins was because she came running down the road towards them, happily yelling, 'I got it! I got it! I got it!'

'Got what?' asked Derrick.

'Not the flu, I hope,' said Boris. 'You aren't the easiest patient to nurse. You always bite my fingers when you get delirious and start thinking they're chocolate brownies.'

'No, I've got something much better than that,' announced Nanny Piggins triumphantly. 'I've got a job.'

'But you've got a job already,' Samantha reminded her.

'You look after us,' said Michael, feeling hurt that his nanny had forgotten.

'Yes, but this is the best job ever in the entire world!' exclaimed Nanny Piggins.

'What?' asked Derrick. 'Has the cake factory in Slimbridge finally answered your letters and given you a job as a cake taster?'

'No, not that,' conceded Nanny Piggins.

'Has the United Nations answered your letters?' asked Michael. 'Are they letting you be in charge of giving World Heritage status to all your favourite cake shops and suppliers?'

'Okay, well it's not quite as good as that, but it's still jolly good. I was reading the newspaper this morning . . .' began Nanny Piggins.

'But you hate reading the newspaper,' protested Samantha, 'because it is full of so many nasty stories about sad people.'

'I know,' agreed Nanny Piggins, 'but it was wrapped around my large serving of chips with extra salt and vinegar, so it was hard for this particular advertisement not to catch my eye.'

'What did it say?' asked Boris.

'The council was advertising for a lollipop lady!' exclaimed Nanny Piggins. 'Can you believe that? And I went for an interview and I got the job! They are actually going to pay me to stand in the street holding a giant lollipop outside the school. It's the perfect job for me because I love licking things generally, but lollipops in particular. And you're all welcome to come and lick it as much as you like before classes begin.'

The children did not know quite what to say.

Samantha, being the most compassionate, spoke first. 'Nanny Piggins, I'm afraid I have some very bad news.' She took her nanny's hand. 'You had better brace yourself for a shock. Lollipop ladies don't hold actual lollipops that you can eat. They just hold lollipop signs.'

'What do you mean?!' asked Nanny Piggins, totally appalled.

'A lollipop sign is just in the shape of a lollipop,' explained Derrick. 'It is made of wood and paint, the same as a regular sign.'

Nanny Piggins gasped. She was speechless. Tears started to well in her eyes.

Boris immediately gave her a big bear hug. 'There there, Sarah, we will help you through this.'

'But it's an outrage!' exclaimed Nanny Piggins, through a faceful of thick bear fur. 'How dare they! I am going to sue the council for false and misleading advertising. It's diabolical, it's entrapment, it's a gross and disgraceful misuse of the word lollipop!'

When they got home Nanny Piggins immediately rang Isabella Dunkhurst for legal advice. And while Ms Dunkhurst was enormously sympathetic to

Nanny Piggins' disappointment, she did not think that they had a strong case when it came to the technical points of law. Nor did she think there was any way that Nanny Piggins could get out of the employment contract she had just signed.

Needless to say, an enormous amount of cake was consumed in the Green house that night as the children and Boris supportively did their best to help Nanny Piggins overcome her bitter disappointment.

The next morning, after a hearty breakfast of chocolate pudding with extra chocolate, Nanny Piggins went to her room to put on her new uniform. Her footsteps were heavy as she trudged upstairs. When she emerged a few minutes later she was wearing a white coat (which Nanny Piggins actually liked because she thought it made her look like an evil scientist), a yellow iridescent vest (which would be useful, the ice-cream van man couldn't pretend not to see her now!) and of course she was holding the lollipop sign. Although she could not bring herself to look at it as it made her want to cry. (When the man from the council had dropped the sign off the night before, Nanny Piggins had sobbed. Until that moment she still had not given up hope that it would be entirely made of hard candy. But after five minutes of desperate licking, even she had to concede that it was definitely made of nothing more delicious than plywood and paint.)

'You look lovely, Sarah!' exclaimed Boris, which was true. Nanny Piggins had a knack for making even the most dowdy council-provided uniform seem tremendously glamorous.

'Yes, I know. But I may well starve to death doing this horrible job,' grumbled Nanny Piggins. 'These pockets aren't nearly big enough to hold a mud cake.'

From the dark smears around the pockets, the children could see that their nanny had certainly made a concerted effort trying to get one in there.

'You'll be all right, Nanny Piggins,' comforted Michael. 'You may not get to eat a giant lollipop but at least you only have to work for one hour in the morning and one hour in the afternoon. That's not bad as far as jobs go.'

'I suppose,' muttered Nanny Piggins, 'but to be reduced to this – directing traffic – like a common street sign. And with no getting blasted out of a cannon or anything! What has my career come to? Oh well, I suppose I should just get on with it.'

And so they got the bus down to the school and waited by the zebra crossing. It was not long before the first child appeared. She was a quiet little girl who liked to get to school early so she could sit in the library and read.

'Hello,' the bookish girl said to Nanny Piggins.

'Hello,' said Nanny Piggins glumly.

'Are you the new lollipop lady?' asked the girl.

'Yes,' said Nanny Piggins sadly. 'And did you realise that this lollipop sign is not really a lollipop?'

'No!' said the bookish girl, appropriately appalled. 'Then why did the old lollipop lady lick her sign all the time?'

'Optimism?' suggested Nanny Piggins. 'Come on, I suppose you want me to help you across the road?'

'Yes, please,' said the bookish girl.

So Nanny Piggins trudged out on to the zebra crossing and held her STOP sign up to the oncoming traffic. The cars obediently drew to a stop and the girl crossed the road. But Nanny Piggins still stood there, blocking the way.

'You're supposed to let the traffic through when there are no children crossing,' called Derrick.

'Oh yes, of course,' said Nanny Piggins, withdrawing her sign and walking to the footpath. But there was more bounce in her step now.

'You know, I think there may be more to this

job than I originally thought,' said Nanny Piggins, a twinkle beginning to emerge in her eye.

'What are you thinking?' worried Samantha.

'Hmm? Oh, just that this could actually be a lot of fun,' said Nanny Piggins. Now she was craning her neck first one way and then the other, looking up and down the street. She spotted what she was looking for when a small child turned the corner. 'Ah, there's another one.' She called out to him, 'You, child – hurry up! Come on, run! Actually, no, don't rush. I'll stop the traffic for you now and make them wait.'

Nanny Piggins leapt back onto the crossing, causing much screeching of brakes as she dramatically stabbed her sign into the road (she had seen an elderly wizard do something similar in a movie recently) and held up her other hand with a snappy flick of the wrist, blocking the peak-hour traffic for several minutes while one poor five-year-old carrying a very heavy backpack (why are maths textbooks so unreasonably heavy?) struggled to the crossing, then across the street. Nanny Piggins glared hard at the motorists, before slowly turning and walking off the crossing herself.

'That was fun,' she said with an excited smile.

'You're not abusing your power, are you, Nanny

Piggins?' asked Derrick. (People often phrase things as questions when they are afraid of phrasing them as accusations.)

'Oh yes, of course I am,' said Nanny Piggins. 'But it will do the motorists good. Everyone is always in such a rush these days; delaying them by a few minutes will help them realise the futility of their meaningless lives.'

'I don't think they will want to realise the futility of their meaningless lives while they are trying to drive to work in the morning,' said Samantha.

'No, but like injections, the things that are good for you are often deeply unpleasant,' said Nanny Piggins. 'Oooh look, here come *two* children. That means I can stop the traffic for twice as long.'

'No, it doesn't,' protested Derrick, as his nanny again burst back onto the crossing.

'It does if I make them cross one at a time for me,' reasoned Nanny Piggins.

And so Nanny Piggins spent a wonderful hour directing traffic. Once she got going she found she had so much to say to the motorists. She told off people for picking their noses when they should have two hands on the steering wheel. She told off people who drove four-wheel drives for driving on the road. To her mind, if you are going to have an off-road vehicle you should drive it *off the road*, so she made them pull up onto the footpath and drive down all the front lawns along the street. And she made all the trucks stop and let her into their cabs so she could pull their horns. Nanny Piggins did enjoy making loud noises.

But the best bit was when the first adult tried to cross the crossing. Nanny Piggins stood, blocking his way.

'Excuse me, I need to get across the road,' said the man politely.

'Of course,' said Nanny Piggins. 'As soon as you give me a lollipop.'

'What?' said the polite man.

'I'm a lollipop lady, and the toll I charge for crossing the road is one lollipop,' explained Nanny Piggins.

'But I've never had to give a lollipop lady a lollipop before,' protested the polite man.

'It's not my fault all the other lollipop ladies don't have any imagination,' said Nanny Piggins.

'But I don't have a lollipop,' complained the polite man.

'That's all right, they sell lots of lovely ones at the corner shop over there. The strawberry ones are particularly good. You should get one for yourself while you're in there,' encouraged Nanny Piggins.

The polite man looked Nanny Piggins in the eye and wisely decided it was best to just do as he was told.

And in this way, Nanny Piggins soon had pocketfuls of lollipops.

Inevitably, forty minutes into Nanny Piggins' shift, when traffic was backed up for five kilometres down the road, and the entire student body was hanging over the front fence watching her performance, Headmaster Pimplestock ventured out to remonstrate with Nanny Piggins. But of course he had no luck. Every time he tried to step into the street, Nanny Piggins would wave the traffic through yelling, 'Go go go!!!' And when he tried to call out to her, Nanny Piggins pretended she could not hear above the noise of the car engines.

At nine o'clock the school bell rang.

'We'd better be going,' said Derrick.

'Well done, Nanny Piggins,' said Samantha encouragingly. 'You got through an entire shift without any children being hit by a car, and the traffic jam is not nearly as bad as when you were trying to get the cars to hit Headmaster Pimplestock.'

'You're right, I think I have a talent for this,' agreed Nanny Piggins.

'Well, we've got to get to class,' said Michael.

'You can't go to school now,' said Nanny Piggins, beginning to pout.

'It is a school day,' Samantha reminded her.

'And the school is right there,' said Michael, pointing to the building not ten metres away.

'And Headmaster Pimplestock has seen us,' added Derrick, 'so it will be difficult to persuade him that we have come down with African Sleeping Sickness today.'

'Yes, but you're on the wrong side of the road,' said Nanny Piggins, 'and it's 9.01 so the lollipop lady has just finished work. You've got no way of getting there.'

'But –' began Samantha.

'She's got a point,' argued Michael. 'It's against school rules to cross without the lollipop lady. And you wouldn't want to break school rules, would you?' He had Samantha there. She was terrified of rule breaking in all its forms.

'But if we don't go to school,' said Derrick, 'what are we going to do?'

'When you've got such a wonderful, powerful sign like this one,' said Nanny Piggins, 'it seems a waste to let it sit around doing nothing for six hours in the middle of the day.'

'But your employment contract very specifically states that you are to direct traffic for one hour before and after the school day,' protested Samantha.

'That's only because they are worried I might have been trying to skive off and do less than they wanted,' said Nanny Piggins. 'I only want to do more. Really they are going to be grateful when they find out how conscientious and dedicated to duty I am.'

And so they started walking towards the centre of town, on the lookout for things to stop with the stop sign. Before long they came to a building site where a crew of workers were demolishing an old house. Nanny Piggins loved heavy machinery, so she leapt out with her stop sign, bringing the entire demolition to a halt, and made the bulldozer driver let her have a go pulling the levers on his machine. She had a wonderful time. Nanny Piggins soon knocked the building down. Admittedly, it was the wrong building, but the bulldozer driver was very kind about it. He said he was impressed with her aptitude for wrecking things.

Next they saw a lawnmower man hard at work, so Nanny Piggins waved her sign at him, bringing him to a halt and asking if they could each have a go on his ride-on lawnmower. He happily agreed, and it was a lot of fun for everyone. It had never occurred to the lawnmower man that he could use his lawnmower to write messages into peoples' lawns (and mowing 'Don't forget to water me!' into the grass was a lot more exciting than just going up and down in straight lines). It soon became apparent that having a lollipop sign was like having free tickets to a fun park.

Finally they made it into town where there was a lot of traffic. Trucks and vans were dropping things off and picking things up from all the local businesses. At first Nanny Piggins did not know where to start. She was tempted to stop a bus and make all the office workers go home to watch daytime television. And she did think about stopping the pizza delivery boy and demanding he took all the anchovies off all his pizzas. But then she saw the most wonderful vehicle ever to roll along a road.

'Look!' cried Nanny Piggins. 'It's a truck from the Slimbridge Cake Factory!'

'Wow!' said Derrick in awe (he particularly loved their lemon cheesecake).

'It's so big!' exclaimed Samantha (she particularly enjoyed their marble cake).

'Just think how many jam rolls they could fit in there,' marvelled Michael (who had a fondness for their jam rolls).

'Wait here,' said Nanny Piggins as she strode out into the road with all the authority of a power-mad lollipop lady who has only been in the job for an hour and a half. She stood in the path of the huge eighteen-wheeler full of cake and held her stop sign forward. The truck's compression brakes hissed and shuddered loudly as the driver brought his vehicle to a halt. Then Nanny Piggins walked around to the cab window and rapped on it.

'Oh, what's she going to do?' worried Samantha.

'I bet she commandeers his vehicle,' said Michael. He did not want his nanny to have to go on the run from the law, but if you are going to go on the run from the law, an eighteen-wheeler full of cake is the vehicle to do it in.

The driver rolled down his window. 'What do you want?' he asked morosely.

'I'd like some cake please,' said Nanny Piggins respectfully. (While she did not have respect for most forms of authority, she did have a great deal of respect for cake. And to her mind a man who drove a cake truck was the highest form of authority there could possibly be. Much more important than headmasters, presidents, prime ministers or members of any royal family.)

The children held their breath waiting for the truck driver to rudely tell Nanny Piggins to go away, but instead he did the most surprising thing. He burst into tears. And watching a fully grown man, with big muscles and tattoos on those muscles, wracking with sobs, is a heartbreaking sight. Nanny Piggins soon had him out of the cab and sitting on the side of the road, while she patted him on the back and fed him reassuring pieces of cake.

'There there, it's all right,' she told him. 'We are great fans of your cake. Whatever your problem is, we promise to help you.'

'It's so dreadful,' sobbed the truck driver. 'I don't want to talk about it.'

'But how can anything be dreadful when you work for the most wonderful institution in the world?' asked Nanny Piggins. 'Your cake factory brings joy to cake lovers everywhere.'

'But that's just it,' explained the truck driver, wiping his nose. 'Everything is changing at the factory . . .' He choked up and couldn't continue speaking.

'You can tell us,' said Nanny Piggins.

'There's a new owner, and she stopped giving the employees free samples,' said the truck driver, starting to sob again.

'She's done what?' asked Nanny Piggins, utterly astounded.

'We used to get free cakes every week as part of our salary,' explained the truck driver, 'and she's put a stop to it.'

Now Nanny Piggins started to cry too, for it was such a desperately sad story.

'And she's changing what the factory makes. She's converting all the machines so they manufacture health bars,' he continued.

Nanny Piggins gasped. 'But can't you have her locked up? She must be criminally insane. Health bars are disgusting.'

'I know.' The truck driver was really blubbering now. 'She made us all eat one.'

Nanny Piggins clutched the truck driver to her chest. 'You poor, poor fellow. Man's inhumanity to cake knows no bounds. Your species can be so cruel sometimes. Don't worry, I'll take care of it.'

'But what can you do?' worried Samantha.

'I've got a stop sign and an iridescent jacket – what can't I do?' said Nanny Piggins boldly. 'As a council-employed lollipop lady it is my job to stop wrongs wherever they are committed.'

'I'm pretty sure that's what superheroes do, not lollipop ladies,' said Derrick.

'Lollipop ladies are better than superheroes,' said Nanny Piggins dismissively. 'Every day lollipop ladies stop hundreds of children being run over by cars, whereas superheroes only save one or two grown adults at a time.'

And so Nanny Piggins and the children got in the truck with the truck driver and drove back to the factory. When they got there they left the truck driver to weep quietly in his cab while Nanny Piggins set out to fight for truth, justice and cake. She marched right onto the factory floor, went up to the first employee she saw and demanded, 'Take me to your leader!'

She then had to repeat the demand, because the employee had earplugs in. But Nanny Piggins was soon taken to see the shop foreman. He was a burly, grouchy-looking man in his early fifties. But Nanny Piggins was not intimidated. (He did not have a lollipop sign.)

'I demand that you immediately stop the production of health bars and return to making the delicious cakes, beloved by all who taste them,' said Nanny Piggins.

The children braced themselves, waiting for the foreman to yell at her. But instead he gave Nanny Piggins a big hug. 'Thank you, thank you so much!' he gushed. 'We've been waiting for someone to lead an uprising. Would you like us all to go out on strike? We've been wanting to ever since she unplugged the machine that makes jam rolls.'

'Oh yes, I think you should immediately go on strike,' urged Nanny Piggins. 'I suggest you take all the cake you can carry over to the park across the street and have a big picnic while I go upstairs and find the managers responsible for these terrible decisions.'

'But, Nanny Piggins, aren't you going too far?' protested Samantha. 'Some people like health food bars. Isn't it wrong to stop the factory from making them? They are healthy.'

'Oh no, they're not,' disagreed the foreman. 'They contain just as much sugar and fat as the cake. The only difference is they taste awful. Oh, and they're good for your bowels.'

'The human obsession with bowels never ceases to amaze me,' said Nanny Piggins, shaking her head. 'I've never understood the attraction of having a fast-acting intestinal system. Some things should not be hurried.'

'That's what I tried to tell management, but they wouldn't listen,' said the foreman.

So the foreman pressed the big bell, letting all the employees know the shift was ending early. Then he let Nanny Piggins press it again, because she was so impressed with the noise. The cheering employees took armfuls of cake off the assembly lines and went out into the sunlight to enjoy themselves, while the children followed Nanny Piggins as she went upstairs to take things in hand.

When the lift opened they stepped out into a big luxurious office suite, but there was no-one about. Except for one receptionist, sitting at her desk scoffing a chocolate mini-muffin.

'Aha!' cried Nanny Piggins.

'It was a health food bar – I swear!' fibbed the receptionist, the crumbs around her mouth giving her away.

'It's all right, we are here to fight for the rights of cake,' declared Nanny Piggins. 'Just tell me where the most senior person is and I'll soon have this sorted out.'

'There's a meeting being held in the boardroom,' said the receptionist, 'but I'm not supposed to allow anybody to interrupt.'

'Don't worry, I'm not just anybody,' said Nanny

Piggins as she strode towards the boardroom. 'I'm the lollipop lady.'

Nanny Piggins flung open the doors, stamped her sign down on the floor and yelled, 'Stop!'

'Who are you? How dare you interrupt our board meeting,' said the angry woman at the head of the table.

'I have come here to tell you to stop the changes you are making to this cake factory,' announced Nanny Piggins.

'It's a "baked goods" factory now,' said the woman.

'Hah!' scoffed Nanny Piggins. 'Madam, there is nothing "good" about your baked products. The traditional cakes made at this factory have brought untold joy to every single person whose lips they pass. You cannot be allowed to stop making them.'

'It's my business!' yelled the owner. 'I paid for it. I'll make what I like!'

'But I'm holding a stop sign!' retorted Nanny Piggins. 'And I'm telling you to stop, or rather stop stop making cakes, which means you have to start making them again, because I say so!'

Fortunately at this point, just as Nanny Piggins was about to abandon reasoned argument and start biting people, the most wonderful thing happened. The receptionist burst in.

'I told you – no interruptions!' screamed the owner. (She really did need a good piece of cake to cheer her up.)

'But there is someone here from the United Nations,' spluttered the receptionist.

'What?' demanded the owner.

'There is an emissary from the United Nations,' explained the receptionist. 'They have brought a certificate for you.'

There was a knock at the door.

'Can we come in, please?' said a voice from the other side. 'Hello, we are from the United Nations. I am delighted to inform you that your factory and the cakes it produces have been given World Heritage status.'

'But we plan to stop baking cakes,' protested the owner.

'Oh no, you can't do that,' smiled the emissary. 'Now that you have World Heritage status, this factory must be protected for future generations. You aren't allowed to change anything, ever.'

'But it's my factory!' whined the owner.

'Yes, but it's our world. And it is important to

protect the most beautiful and culturally significant things in it,' he explained. 'The Secretary-General himself made sure that the paperwork on this factory was pushed through quickly.'

'Why?' asked the owner, totally amazed.

'Apparently,' explained the emissary, 'he got a very sternly worded letter from a former flying pig demanding that he did so.'

Nanny Piggins smiled. 'You have to have a firm hand with these authority figures. But if you tell them what to do, they usually respond.'

'Normally the Secretary-General would have crumpled up the letter and thrown it in the bin,' continued the emissary. 'But there was a piece of cake included in the envelope, and when he tasted it he realised the pig was right. So he rushed to fill out the paperwork.'

'I put in a slice of your triple chocolate fudge cake,' explained Nanny Piggins. 'I knew any man who spent all day every day trying to achieve world peace could do with a slice of cake.'

The owner took the certificate declaring the World Heritage listing of her factory and slumped in defeat. 'But I had such plans for the factory. The previous owners spent so much money buying quality ingredients, the profit margins were terrible.'

'Don't worry,' said the emissary. 'You're going to make plenty of profit. For a start the Secretary-General wants to order one million of your chocolate fudge cakes to drop over international trouble spots. He thinks people will be less likely to fight all the time if they've got more sugar in their diets.'

'What a brilliant man,' admired Nanny Piggins. 'I wish I'd voted for him.'

'You don't vote for a Secretary-General,' explained Derrick. 'He's appointed.'

'Ah, that makes sense,' nodded Nanny Piggins. 'Nobody democratically elected would ever be that sensible.'

And so the truck driver took Nanny Piggins and the children home. As they drove out the gates, the staff from the factory cheered and threw their cake in the air (then carefully caught it again so they could eat more).

When they got home, there was a message on the phone saying that Nanny Piggins was fired from her job as the lollipop lady because she had entirely missed her afternoon shift. Headmaster Pimplestock had had to go out and direct the traffic himself, and since there were no men's uniforms, he had had to wear a white dress and lady's hat, which only made the students laugh at him even more than usual.

'I'm sorry you lost your job, Nanny Piggins,' sympathised Michael.

'It's all right. It's a relief really. These stop signs carry too much power. It's fine for one day. But if I had one all the time, I'd hate to become a despot,' said Nanny Piggins.

And so Nanny Piggins and the children settled down to celebrate her return to single employment with some of the many thank-you cakes given to them by the employees of the Slimbridge Cake Factory. It is amazing how much cake will accidentally fall off the back of a truck into your waiting arms when the truck driver purposefully does very tight figure-of-eight turns in the street outside your house trying to make it do just that.

CHAPTER 5

Coach Green

'Don't do it, Nanny Piggins!' cried Samantha.

'Please don't jump!' begged Derrick.

'Ung-uhuh-boohoo-hoo,' sobbed Boris.

The children and Boris were standing in the middle of the backyard looking up at the roof, where Nanny Piggins stood on the ridgepole with her arms raised, sniffing the breeze, ready to leap. You see, Nanny Piggins had been watching a fascinating documentary. She normally disliked documentaries (she resented anything that tried to educate in slow, measured tones) and would have switched it off before it started but she was eating a particularly good cream bun at the time so her hands were too sticky to change the channel. Anyway, the documentary had been about the Pentecost Islanders in Vanuatu, who just happened to be the people who invented bungy jumping.

Now on Pentecost Island, the local people jump off a purpose-built scaffold with nothing but vines tied to their ankles to stop them hitting the ground. Nanny Piggins did not have any vines to hand, so she had to make do. She cut the elastic out of all of Mr Green's underpants and wove them into one long bungy cord (rest assured, she had thoroughly laundered them first).

This cord was now tied to her ankles at one end and the TV aerial on the roof at the other. This is probably sounding incredibly dangerous to you, but Nanny Piggins was not a silly pig. As an additional safety measure she had borrowed Mrs Lau's above-ground pool (Mrs Lau was down at the church hall playing bingo, so Nanny Piggins was sure she would not mind). The pool was there for Nanny Piggins to fall into if she had made a mistake in her calculations and overestimated the elasticity of Mr Green's underpants.

Nevertheless, the children and Boris were anxious. Samantha was concerned that Nanny Piggins might miss the pool entirely. Derrick was concerned that she would fall down and then spring back up and bang her head on the roof gable. And Michael was concerned that she would do both. (Nobody knew what Boris' concerns were, because he was weeping too hard to be able to articulate them.)

'You can't jump, Nanny Piggins,' urged Michael. 'Think of the consequences.'

'Pish!' said Nanny Piggins. 'The worst that could happen is I break my leg. And since I've got four of those, it would only be half as bad as a human breaking their leg.'

'No, something much more terrible could happen,' said Samantha, trying to appeal to her nanny's way of thinking. 'If your head landed in the pool – your hair would be ruined!'

This did make Nanny Piggins pause and think, as she was having a particularly lovely hair day.

'Hmm, you make a good point,' admitted Nanny Piggins, 'but sometimes sacrifices need to be made. If I am going to be open to new and exciting cultural experiences I'll just have to risk having damp hair.'

'Yes, but something even worse than that could happen,' argued Derrick.

'Piffle!' said Nanny Piggins. 'What could possibly be worse than having unattractive hair?'

'You might damage the television aerial,' said Derrick.

Nanny Piggins turned and looked at the television aerial – the wondrous technological device that captured electromagnetic waves from the air to bring *The Young and the Irritable* and *The Bold and the Spiteful* into their home every day. A tear came to Nanny Piggins' eye as she realised what she had so nearly done. 'Oh my goodness, you're right,' said Nanny Piggins. 'What was I thinking? How could I endanger the source of so much of our happiness? I'll climb down immediately.'

Unfortunately that was not to be. Because just as Nanny Piggins bent down to untie her improvised bungy cords, she heard a loud whistle blast. When she looked up she saw Mr Green in the backyard with a whistle in his mouth, wearing a brand new tracksuit. Nanny Piggins was so shocked she immediately toppled off the roof and plummeted towards Mrs Lau's pool.

'Oh no!' wailed Samantha, hoping her father's underwear was as reliable as the vines of Vanuatu.

'She's going to get wet,' predicted Michael.

And he was right. Nanny Piggins splashed headfirst into the water. Fortunately the water was 130 centimetres deep and Nanny Piggins was only 120 centimetres tall, so while she was completely submerged for a second, her head did not touch the bottom.

When the bungy cord contracted and yanked Nanny Piggins skywards again, she looked up, blinking water out of her eyes. And Nanny Piggins was shocked to see that she had not been imagining it – Mr Green really was wearing a tracksuit. Fortunately the surprised expletive she uttered was silenced as the bungee cord stretched out again and she plunged headfirst back into the water.

Minutes later, after Nanny Piggins had bounced up and down several times, the children rescued her from the bungy cord. Samantha and Michael had to wade into the pool and hold Nanny Piggins' head above the water while Derrick climbed up on the roof and cut the cord off the television aerial. (Only minor damage was done to the aerial, so they would still be able to enjoy *The Young and the Irritable*. It's just that now all the actors' faces were blue where they should be pink and their clothes were pink where they should be blue. But when a program is as exciting as *The Young and the Irritable* you are never going to notice a little thing like that.)

During the melee Boris used the opportunity to leap into the pool and hide. Fortunately he had a drinking straw stuck to his fur from a milkshake he had enjoyed earlier, so by breathing through the straw, he was able to stay underwater and thus avoid detection.

As soon as Nanny Piggins was standing upright on her own trotters, she confronted Mr Green. 'What do you think you are doing?' she demanded.

'I have every right to stand in my own backyard,' said Mr Green petulantly.

'I know that,' said Nanny Piggins. 'I mean what are you doing wearing a tracksuit?'

'You never exercise,' added Derrick.

'You never wear comfortable clothes,' agreed Samantha.

'I've never seen you wear anything but a three-piece suit before,' observed Michael.

'Even when the weather is unseasonably hot and you come home from work smelling like old gym socks, you still wear the same suit,' said Nanny Piggins.

'It's none of your business,' snapped Mr Green. Then he realised that the opposite was in fact true. 'Well, actually, it does involve you. I have volunteered to coach your soccer team.'

The children and Nanny Piggins stared at Mr Green for a moment, not knowing what to say. Fortunately for Mr Green it was his politest child who gathered her thoughts and spoke first. 'But, Father, we aren't in a soccer team,' said Samantha.

'What do you mean?' asked Mr Green.

Derrick tried to explain the situation to his father, slowly and clearly, as if he were a half-witted foreign tourist (as indeed he was whenever he went overseas). 'We – do – not – belong – to – a – soccer – team.'

'Ridiculous!' spluttered Mr Green. 'All children play soccer. I've seen them running around on playing fields wearing uniforms.'

'We don't,' said Michael, 'because Nanny Piggins doesn't believe in organised sport.'

Nanny Piggins nodded at the truth of this. 'I don't believe in organised anything, but sport in particular. The rules ruin the fun. Did you know that even in boxing, there are rules against biting? Now how can you enjoy any game where you're not allowed to bite your opponent's shins?'

Mr Green looked like he was about to throw some sort of tantrum. He went red in the face and his neck started to wobble. 'But I've just volunteered to coach the local team!'

'Why on earth did you do that?' asked Nanny Piggins.

'The Father of the Year Competition!' exclaimed Mr Green, unable to say any more because he was so upset. But this was all the information they needed.

'Aaaaah,' said Nanny Piggins and the children knowingly.

'I had to do something!' blustered Mr Green. 'Smythe in Accounts took his daughter on a three-day canoeing holiday; Thorp in Corporate Law didn't have any children so he adopted three from Africa and took them to the zoo; and Peterson from Criminal Law took his sons hiking in Papua New Guinea! And if the tribesman ever free him he's sure to get the prize unless I do something to make myself stand out.'

'So you let everyone at work know you were volunteering to coach your children's soccer team?' guessed Nanny Piggins.

Mr Green nodded. 'I thought it would be the easiest thing to do. I didn't want to commit to anything that involves taking malaria tablets.'

'But, Father,' said Derrick kindly, 'do you even know anything about soccer?'

'Of course I do!' said Mr Green. 'You kick a ball about. It isn't complicated.'

'Yes, but in soccer you kick a *soccer ball* about, not a *basketball*,' said Michael, looking meaningfully at the kit bag full of basketballs at Mr Green's feet.

'What's the difference?!' protested Mr Green. 'They're all round, aren't they?'

'Never mind, I'm sure your boss will be impressed when he finds out you coach a soccer team that doesn't even have your own children in it,' said Nanny Piggins, turning back to the house. 'Come along, children, let's have another go at bungy jumping.'

'No, no, no!' said Mr Green petulantly. 'That will not do. It is bad enough I have to coach a team. I don't want to coach other people's children!'

'Because you won't be able to bully them the way you bully your own children?' guessed Nanny Piggins correctly.

'I am not coaching it unless you three are in the team!' said Mr Green adamantly. 'You will all have to sign up immediately. And that's that!'

'You can't make them,' said Nanny Piggins.

'Yes I can, I'll dock their –' began Mr Green,

but then he remembered he did not give his children any pocket money that he could dock. 'I won't take them to –' started Mr Green, but again, he had to stop mid-threat because he remembered he never took his children anywhere. 'I won't allow them to have –' He soon realised that threat would not work either because he never let them have anything.

'Perhaps if you bribed them,' suggested Nanny Piggins.

'I will not bribe my own children,' spluttered Mr Green.

'I don't see why not,' said Nanny Piggins. 'No child's bedroom would ever be cleaned if it weren't for the compelling effects of a confectionary bribe.'

'You'll join the team if I supply you with some chocolate?' asked Mr Green, beginning to catch on (goodness knows why he was so slow on the uptake because all his negotiations with Nanny Piggins always came back to this).

'It would have to be a lot of chocolate,' said Derrick. (His nanny had trained him well in the art of negotiating.)

'Three large family-sized bars each!' declared Nanny Piggins.

'Why do you need three?' protested Mr Green.

'One for each meal of the day,' explained Nanny Piggins.

'But Nanny Piggins,' said Michael, 'you're forgetting morning tea and afternoon tea.'

'Goodness, you're right, you'd better make it five blocks each,' said Nanny Piggins.

'And five blocks for Nanny Piggins as well,' added Samantha, 'because she'll be our personal trainer.'

'No, it would have to be ten blocks for Nanny Piggins,' said Derrick. 'Her metabolism is much faster.'

Nanny Piggins nodded at the truth of this.

'But that's twenty-five blocks of chocolate!' wailed Mr Green.

'Either that or you call a casting agency and you hire actors to play your children again,' said Nanny Piggins.

'What do you mean "again"?' asked Mr Green shiftily.

'I know the things you do to drive to work in the transit lane,' said Nanny Piggins, giving Mr Green a piercing glare.

'All right, all right, I agree to it all,' said Mr Green, taking out his cheque book. 'The first practice session is tonight. You had better all be there.'

'Hmm, we should be able to make it,' said Nanny Piggins, watching closely as Mr Green filled in the cheque (just in case he tried using a false name). 'Although we will be twenty minutes late because we will have to go down to the sweet shop and get the chocolate first.'

When Nanny Piggins and the children arrived at the soccer field, it was immediately apparent that Mr Green was desperately out of his depth. He was standing on his own, away from the small gaggle of children, looking petrified.

'What have we missed?' asked Nanny Piggins.

'Nothing,' whispered Mr Green. 'They haven't done anything yet.'

'You do realise that you're the coach, and you're supposed to tell them what to do?' asked Nanny Piggins.

'What?' exclaimed Mr Green. 'I thought it was just my job to bring the balls and call an ambulance if one of them breaks a wrist. I was planning to spend my time sitting in the Rolls Royce doing paperwork.'

'No, Father, a coach is actually meant to do coaching,' explained Samantha.

'You have to run drills, explain tactics, and generally teach the team how to play soccer,' added Michael.

'I have to speak to them?' said Mr Green disbelievingly.

His children nodded.

Mr Green's shoulders slumped as he trudged over to talk to his young soccer team. 'Ahem,' he began, clearing his throat. 'All right, well then, let's see, to start with . . .'

'You're not being paid by the hour now, get on with it,' heckled Nanny Piggins.

'All right. Run round the field ten times!' ordered Mr Green.

The children set off. And even though running around a sports field is one of the most physically painful and awfully boring things children are regularly forced to do, they were actually relieved to not have to stand there looking at Mr Green anymore. Plus it was a cold night and they desperately needed to do something to warm up.

Nanny Piggins left Mr Green to it. She went over to the sidelines where she set up a camping stove and got to work making hot chocolate for when the practice session was over. It was a pleasant way to while away a couple of hours. Making hot chocolate, testing it until it was all gone, then making more. All while watching Mr Green make a complete twit of himself.

Once the children finished running (Mr Green had not kept count, so they got away with only doing three laps), Mr Green started by trying to demonstrate how to dribble the ball. But he had no idea how to do it, so he tripped over several times: first over the ball, then over his own feet, then over Michael's foot (because Michael could not resist sticking it out as his father lumbered past).

Next Mr Green tried teaching the children how to shoot for goal. You never would have imagined that a fully grown man could find it so difficult to get something as small as a basketball into something as large as a soccer goal. But after seventy-nine attempts Mr Green gave up and grumbled, 'Well, you get the general idea,' and let the children have a go.

The practice eventually drew to a close five minutes before scheduled time when the last of the basketballs was lost into the river running alongside the oval. (They had already lost two into oncoming traffic on the street, three into unclimbable trees, one into the blades of a passing helicopter and one to a local hoodlum who simply caught it and ran off.)

Then the children got their first enjoyable exercise for the night when Mr Green blew his whistle twice, announcing practice had finished, and they all ran over to Nanny Piggins for hot chocolate. (Nanny Piggins made a mental note to put Mr Green's whistle under the tyre of his Rolls Royce before he backed out of the driveway the next morning.)

'Well, children, I hope that wasn't too dreadful,' sympathised Nanny Piggins.

'It was fun to see Father try to run,' admitted Derrick.

'I liked the new words Mr Green taught us when he fell over,' said Samson Wallace. (He and his sister, Margaret, were in the team because Nanny Anne scheduled them to have seven hours of outdoor exercise per week.)

'Yes, you must be sure to use one or two of those words on Nanny Anne as soon as you get home,' suggested Nanny Piggins naughtily.

'Well, I thought that went rather well,' said Mr Green as he limped over to join them. (He did not want to speak to any of them, but he could not resist the smell of hot chocolate. Plus, he supposed, with the Father of the Year Competition being so close and the weather being so cold, he probably should offer his children a lift home.) 'I think we're ready for our first match on Saturday morning.'

'You expect us to play a match?!' exclaimed Samantha.

'Against another team?!' asked Derrick.

'And on Saturday morning when all the good cartoons are on?!' asked Nanny Piggins, deeply shocked.

'Of course,' said Mr Green. 'That's how a soccer league works.'

'I'm sorry, children,' apologised Nanny Piggins. 'I would have insisted on twenty chocolate bars each if I'd known that joining a soccer team would have such dreadful ramifications.'

When their father dropped them off at home, barely slowing down the car long enough for them to get out before speeding off back to his law office, the children were finally able to talk freely with Nanny Piggins.

'How do you think the game is going to go on Saturday?' asked Derrick.

'I'm sure you'll be fine,' said Nanny Piggins warmly.

The children just looked at her.

'I do,' said Nanny Piggins. 'You all know how

to play soccer. We play it in the house all the time when it's raining.'

'Yes, but that's soccer played to Nanny Piggins' rules,' said Samantha.

'It bears more resemblance to cage-fighting than actual soccer,' agreed Michael.

'Well, the team you're playing might be worse than you,' suggested Nanny Piggins.

'Do you think that's likely?' asked Derrick.

'Anything is possible,' said Nanny Piggins. 'The players in the other team might all have terrible head colds, or dreadful vertigo that makes them dizzy and fall over a lot. Or a huge flood could wash the sports field away entirely, so we can stay home and play pirates. It's always best to be optimistic.'

But on Saturday morning when they arrived at the match they were disappointed to discover that there had been no natural disasters during the night, and the sports ground was still intact. They soon realised that the next ninety minutes were going to be awful, because the other team were clearly a lot more athletic. They wove back and forth, kicking balls around with the precision and grace of synchronised swimmers.

Also the other team were all a lot bigger and a lot taller. It seems Mr Green, not knowing the age of any of his children when he went to sign up, had simply guessed. As a result they were in the under 14s competition when they should have been in the under 12s. And, thanks to testosterone and other growth-related hormones, the difference in size between a twelve-year-old and a fourteen-year-old is huge.

'Oh my goodness, we're going to be slaughtered,' said Samantha.

'No, you're not! There's no way a children's sports league would be allowed to set up an impromptu abattoir in the middle of a game!' said Nanny Piggins, looking about nervously. (Talk of slaughter and abattoirs made any pig anxious.)

'Samantha just means we're going to be beaten,' said Derrick.

'At playing soccer,' added Michael. 'I don't think they'll beat us with sticks. At least not when anyone is looking . . .'

'Hmm,' said Nanny Piggins. 'My advice is this – Derrick and Michael, stay as far away from the ball as possible.'

'What about me?' panicked Samantha.

'Run, run now and hide in the girls' toilets,' urged Nanny Piggins.

Samantha took off, running like the wind. (The tragedy is that if she'd had a proper coach who had taught her how to run that fast while dribbling the ball, she would have been immediately signed up by Manchester United.)

Ninety humiliating minutes later, Mr Green's team lost 189 to 1. (And their one goal was not even scored by them. It was an own goal, scored when one of their opponents was celebrating so hard he accidentally kicked the ball into the wrong net.) When the children came off the field they did not even get the telling off from Mr Green they were expecting. He was so horrified by the awfulness of his team he had gone over to the other side of the pitch and was pretending to be one of the opposition spectators.

'Mr Green, come over here and speak to your team immediately!' demanded Nanny Piggins in a loud carrying voice.

Mr Green looked about as though he did not know who she was talking to.

'Don't make me come over there and get you,' Nanny Piggins warned.

Mr Green hung his head and trudged back to where his team stood. He did not like being dragged by Nanny Piggins. It hurt the back of his head to be scraped along the ground, and it took him forever to fix the bite marks on his trousers using his desk stapler. Mr Green turned to look at the poor, exhausted, bruised and beaten children.

'Well, look here you er . . . children. This really isn't good enough,' blathered Mr Green. 'When I signed up to coach this team it was on the clear understanding, although not precisely stated but obviously implied, that I would in no way be publicly humiliated . . .'

'What is he saying?' Nanny Piggins asked Derrick.

'I think he said we embarrassed him,' explained Derrick.

'What?!' exploded Nanny Piggins, interrupting Mr Green mid-waffle.

'I – er . . .' said Mr Green, desperately trying to work out what had caused his nanny to take offence.

'How dare you say that these poor children have embarrassed *you*?!' ranted Nanny Piggins. 'You, sir, are the embarrassment. You don't know how to play soccer. You don't know how to coach soccer. You don't even know how to go into a shop and buy a soccer ball!'

Nanny Piggins was just working herself up into a full rant when Mr Green silenced her by suddenly and unexpectedly bursting into tears.

'What am I going to do?' wailed Mr Green.

There is something especially pitiful about watching a fully grown man (wearing a tracksuit over a three-piece suit) cry, so that even Nanny Piggins relented.

'Pull yourself together, it's just a children's soccer league. It doesn't matter if they win or lose,' said Nanny Piggins. 'They are just supposed to be having fun and getting exercise.'

'But,' sobbed Mr Green, 'I invited the Senior Partner to come and watch next week's game.'

'Well that was silly,' said Nanny Piggins.

'And I told him they were the best team in the league,' wept Mr Green.

'It's wrong to lie,' chastised Samantha.

'What am I going to do?' wailed Mr Green.

Nanny Piggins sighed. 'You'd better fetch your cheque book.'

'I can't afford to fly in short professional football-ers. I know, I looked into it,' spluttered Mr Green.

'No, but you can afford to buy 100 family-sized bars of chocolate,' said Nanny Piggins.

'Why on earth would I do that?' asked Mr Green.

'To bribe me to coach the team for you,' explained Nanny Piggins.

Mr Green immediately stopped crying and clutched Nanny Piggins by the trotter. 'Oh, would you? Thank you, thank you so much.'

'You'd better run to your car and fetch your cheque book quickly before I change my mind,' warned Nanny Piggins.

And so when the next practice session came around it was Nanny Piggins who was wearing the tracksuit. She still made Mr Green come. It was his job to hand out doughnuts (she did not trust him to make hot chocolate) and sit quietly in the corner, not speaking unless spoken to.

'All right, children,' said Nanny Piggins, addressing her team. 'Soccer is a complicated game. There are a lot of skills involving ducking and weaving. And lots of tactics involving strategy and thinking. All of which would take months, if not years, to learn, and which would be very boring for all of us. I do, however, know an awful lot about projectiles. Blasting things, usually me, enormous distances is my area of expertise. So we will win the game on Saturday because tonight I am going to teach you how to kick the living daylights out of a soccer ball. Do you understand?'

'No,' said all the children in unison.

'That doesn't matter. Understanding is entirely overrated,' said Nanny Piggins. 'Now, have you all brought along the pictures as I instructed?' She had told all the children to bring along a photograph or drawing of the person they most detested in the entire world.

'Yes,' said Samantha. (She had a picture of her maths teacher in her pocket.)

'What do you need them for?' asked Derrick. (He had a picture of Barry Nichols, the school bully.)

'I'll demonstrate,' said Nanny Piggins. 'Samson, did you bring along that picture of Nanny Anne I asked for?'

'Yes,' said Samson. 'I've got one of her accepting a certificate from the Guinness Book of Records for getting the most starch into one pair of underpants.'

'Perfect,' said Nanny Piggins. 'Now, children, watch closely as I use some sticky tape to attach this picture to a soccer ball.'

The children watched Nanny Piggins. They had not been expecting to get an impromptu craft lesson.

'I will place the ball on the ground so that Nanny Anne is looking at me, then take a few steps back. Now, this is the important bit – I shall stare hard at Nanny Anne's face . . .' Nanny Piggins glared at the photograph so fiercely that the few children who had been foolish enough to turn and look at her instead of at the ball had to flinch away in fear, '... concentrating all my feelings of anger and resentment, pushing them down, deep down into my foot ...' Nanny Piggins was silent for a moment while she pushed her feelings. 'And now I shall give Nanny Anne the good kick she deserves!'

Nanny Piggins ran forward and kicked the ball. Or rather she launched the ball. And because she kicked it so hard, it looked and sounded like it had been blasted out of a cannon. The black and white ball flew the entire length of the soccer field and disappeared into the darkness of the night.

'Wow!' said Derrick.

'How do you do that?' asked Michael.

'She really is a very annoying woman,' explained Nanny Piggins.

'But we'll never be able to kick like that,' said Samantha.

'Of course you will. Nanny Anne is annoying but she has never tried to teach me integers. I should imagine your feelings for your maths teacher are even stronger,' said Nanny Piggins. 'Come along, everyone take out your photographs and use the sticky tape to attach them to a ball.'

The rest of the practice session went brilliantly. Young children are such easy targets for bullies, that every member of the team had lots of pent-up emotion towards some spiteful adult or cruel child. Balls were soon flying the length and breadth of the field. When Samantha remembered the time they had studied quadratic equations, she kicked the ball so hard she actually cracked one of the goal posts.

And so the day of the big match arrived. The Green children's confidence began to waver when they saw the size and athleticism of their opponents.

'What are we going to do?' asked Samantha. 'We can't dribble or weave, we don't know any set plays and the referee will never let us stick eleven different photographs to the soccer ball before we start play.'

'Nine different photos,' Derrick reminded her. 'Three of us had photographs of Barry Nichols.'

'You'll be fine,' said Nanny Piggins with complete confidence. 'Tactics are just for people who haven't got the skill to really kick the ball properly.'

'Here he comes, here he comes!' squealed Mr Green excitedly, as he saw the Senior Partner's car pull up.

'What did I tell you about not speaking until you are spoken to?' asked Nanny Piggins sternly.

'Sorry,' mouthed Mr Green silently.

'Ah, Green,' said the Senior Partner. 'Is this your team?'

Mr Green looked at Nanny Piggins to see if he had permission to speak. She nodded. 'Yes,' said Mr Green proudly. (He was not a great conversationalist.)

'I look forward to seeing you all play,' said the Senior Partner, smiling broadly at the children, 'but remember the most important thing is that you have fun playing with your friends.'

'No,' said Margaret Wallace, 'Nanny Piggins says the most important thing is that we have fun kicking our enemies.'

The Senior Partner's brow creased as he puzzled over this statement. But he did not get an opportunity to ask any questions because at that moment the referee blew his whistle to start the game and the children jogged onto the field.

At first Mr Green's team were indeed outplayed. Their opponents wove around them and effortlessly passed back and forth to score a classic goal. But that is where they made their big mistake. You see after you score a goal, the other team gets to take the ball back to the middle and kick off again.

This was Samantha's job, so she was standing at the halfway line thinking dark thoughts about her maths teacher, waiting for the referee to get in position. She did not hear the taunts from the other team of 'It's just a girl' and 'Let's get her'. She was too busy taking all her repressed rage and pushing it down into her foot. As soon as she registered the sound of the whistle she leapt forward and slammed her boot into the ball using every ounce of strength in her body.

The ball flew the length of the field, slamming into the opposition goalkeeper. It hit him so hard in the stomach he doubled over and stumbled backwards, collapsing on the ground so the ball rolled off his stomach into the net. And that is how Mr Green's team scored their first goal.

From that point on it was a bloodbath. Mr Green's team were blasting the soccer ball at the goal as if they had bazookas for legs. In the end, the opposition team forfeited the game at halftime because two of their players had broken kneecaps (their fault for standing in front of Margaret Wallace when she was shooting for goal) and the rest of them were too afraid to go back on the field again.

'Well, Green,' said the Senior Partner, 'you've done some extraordinary work with these children. They're a pretty weedy bunch to look at, but you've certainly taught them how to kick.'

'Thank you, thank you so much, sir,' grovelled Mr Green. 'Please allow me to run and fetch you an ice-cream from the kiosk.'

'Okay, but shouldn't you be getting ice-cream for all your team for winning their game?' asked the Senior Partner.

Mr Green gulped. He instinctively disliked doing nice things for children. 'Oh no, I think they're all lactose intolerant,' he lied.

'They are not,' said Nanny Piggins. 'They'll all have three-scoop cones with a scoop of chocolate, a scoop of chocolate-chip and a scoop of chocolate with choc-chips.'

'You heard the lady,' laughed the Senior Partner.

Mr Green ran off to do as he was told.

'But I suspect I should really be congratulating Green on his ability to delegate to a certain glamorous assistant coach,' said the Senior Partner, winking at Nanny Piggins.

'I don't know what you're talking about,' said Nanny Piggins, although her blush gave her away.

CHAPTER 6

Nanny Piggins Stands Accused

It was April Fools' Day, so Nanny Piggins and the children were baking biscuits in the shape of letters from the alphabet. This may seem like an unexpectedly educational thing to do, but the only reason they were making the letters was so Nanny Piggins could send Headmaster Pimplestock a rude message. She thought this was a tremendously funny idea. And how could the headmaster complain when he received an insult in the form of 812 delicious sugar-coated shortbread cookies. (Nanny Piggins had thought up quite a long rude message.)

Unfortunately, just as they were sprinkling icing sugar over the warm biscuits, their festive activity was interrupted by the sound of a helicopter overhead. Now you are probably thinking – why would the sound of a helicopter interrupt a baking session? That is because you are thinking of the noise a helicopter makes when it is a long way overhead. But trust me, when a helicopter is hovering just thirty metres directly above your house it makes a noise so loud that all the furniture shakes, the crockery rattles and conversation becomes impossible.

'What's going on?!' yelled Nanny Piggins as she bent over the cookies. Just in case the house did collapse, she wanted to shield the biscuits with her body. (Spending two days trapped in the rubble of a building would not be so bad if you had 812 biscuits to keep you company.)

Just then, the helicopter pulled away and there was an even louder sound, a voice bellowing from outside, 'Nanny Piggins, we have the house surrounded. Come out with your hands up!'

'I don't know what to do, children,' said Nanny Piggins. 'Normally I never like to obey anyone who does not say "please". But I am ever so curious to know why they have surrounded the house.'

'Would you like us to hide you in the cellar until they go away?' asked Michael. 'We could build a secret wall and you could live as a recluse.'

'Hmm, tempting as that does sound because the heroine in the Regency Romance novel I've just been reading did a very similar thing,' mused Nanny Piggins, 'I think I'd prefer to answer the door. I bet it is just someone we know playing a lovely practical joke. And the sooner we answer the door, the sooner I can play my own practical joke back, by biting them on the leg.'

And so Nanny Piggins and the children went to the front door fully expecting lots of laughing and joking and perhaps a pie fight to follow. They were soon to be bitterly disappointed, because when they threw open the door there was no smiling face. Just the grim expression of the Police Sergeant standing on the doorstep. And looking past him, they could see a dozen police patrol cars blocking the street with police officers cowering behind them.

'Hello, Nanny Piggins,' said the Police Sergeant.

He was not looking his normal happy self this morning.

'Hello, Police Sergeant,' said Nanny Piggins. 'Have you naughty boys from the police station decided to play an April Fools' trick on me? Well, it is a lovely thought. And I am flattered. But shouldn't you have left some of your officers at the station in case a real crime happens.'

'A real crime has happened,' said the Police Sergeant.

'Oh dear, and so early in the day. Poor you, Sergeant. I know you are not a morning person. Would you like a biscuit?' asked Nanny Piggins. 'I am prepared to edit the rude message I am writing to Headmaster Pimplestock because your need does seem greater.'

'I'm afraid I can't,' said the Police Sergeant.

'Really?' said Nanny Piggins, very surprised. 'But you love my butter shortbread biscuits.'

The Police Sergeant sniffed the air. The biscuits did smell good. But then he remembered why he had come and girded himself. 'I can't eat your biscuits because I have come here to arrest you,' he said. 'Sorry,' he added as an afterthought, because he really was a very polite policeman.

The children were horrified.

'But you can't arrest Nanny Piggins,' protested Derrick, 'because, because . . .' (He struggled here because he knew his nanny well, so he knew that there were actually several dozen reasons why the Police Sergeant probably *should* arrest her.)

'You can't arrest her because we won't let you!' declared Samantha boldly, standing in front of her nanny with her arms outstretched.

'It's all right, Samantha,' said Nanny Piggins. 'The Police Sergeant is only joking. Men in uniform are always such tremendous pranksters. The helicopter overhead, the twelve police cars and the snipers I can see on Mrs Lau's roof are all just part of a very elaborate practical joke. We should play along with it, it will be fun.'

'I don't think so, Nanny Piggins,' worried Michael (and he was not a child normally given to worrying). 'Snipers aren't known for their sense of humour.'

'Pish!' said Nanny Piggins. 'It would be rude not to play along when they have gone to so much trouble. All right, Police Sergeant,' she said, winking at him as she offered up her wrists to be handcuffed, 'why don't you take me downtown and throw the book at me.'

And so the Police Sergeant was able to take

Nanny Piggins down to the station without her escaping in a cannon blast, swinging from building to building using her trapeze skills, disguising herself as a sanitation worker and disappearing into the sewers, or any of the other brilliant things he had imagined she might do.

It was only when she was down at the station and the Police Sergeant had the audacity to fingerprint her trotters, using ink that did not easily wash off with soap, that Nanny Piggins first began to suspect this was either a very poorly thought through practical joke, or she had really just been arrested. At this point she got very cross, and chased all the police officers around and around the station, giving them each several nasty bites on the leg and stamping on their feet. Eventually they were able to trap her in a cell (by throwing in a packet of chocolate biscuits, then slamming the door closed behind her when she instinctively lunged after them).

By the time the children had fetched Boris and caught the bus down to the police station, Nanny Piggins was a very sad pig indeed. Fortunately she was able to buck herself up by eating three or four hundred of the biscuits that the children had brought in for her. (The rude message to Headmaster Pimplestock would have to wait for another day.)

'So why have they arrested you? What did you do?' asked Samantha.

'I didn't do anything!' protested Nanny Piggins, stuffing another two dozen biscuits in her mouth in an effort to control her rage.

'No, of course not,' comforted Derrick, 'but what do they think you did?'

'They are saying I broke into the Natural History Museum and stole the Giant Mumbai Diamond – which I certainly did not!' said Nanny Piggins angrily, rattling the bars of her cell.

'Oh, I read about that in the paper,' said Samantha, 'but it happened on Monday night, so it can't have been you. That was the night you spent in Mrs Simpson's attic trying to catch her possum.'

'I know! That's what I told the police,' exclaimed Nanny Piggins, 'but they say they are unable to verify my alibi.'

'What does that mean?' asked Michael.

'Mrs Simpson won't back her up,' explained Derrick.

'I probably should have told her that's what I was doing,' said Nanny Piggins regretfully. 'She says she heard a lot of banging and crashing, and saw a foot stamp through the ceiling. But she thought it was just her dead husband's ghost, haunting her for forgetting to water his geraniums.'

'But why did they arrest *you*?' asked Michael. 'If a giant chocolate cake had gone missing, I could see why you might be a suspect. But it's not like you have a criminal record for stealing the world's most valuable diamonds. You don't, do you?'

'Of course not!' said Nanny Piggins. 'No, they have arrested me because they have a witness who says he saw me.'

'A witness!' exclaimed the children.

'But what sort of mean sneaking low-life would dob someone in for a crime she did not commit?' asked Boris.

'I don't know,' said Nanny Piggins, 'but there is going to be a line-up this afternoon where the witness has to pick me out. Which, under normal circumstances, would be thrilling because whenever I've seen line-ups in police programs I've always wanted to be in one so I could bite the real criminal. But it's not so thrilling now there is a prospect of me being identified as the real criminal.'

'Never mind,' said Boris reassuringly. 'I'm sure it's all just a horrible mistake and the witness won't be able to pick you out. It was probably one of those incredibly glamorous supermodels who did it. You look so much like them, it would be an easy mistake to make.'

A short time later, Nanny Piggins was led into a room and asked to line up against the wall between four bedraggled-looking women.

Meanwhile in the next room, behind a two-way mirror, the witness was lead in to view the line-up.

'All right sir, rest assured they can't see you, so take your time,' began the Police Sergeant.

'It's her, it's her, it's the pig in the middle!' cried the witness before he'd barely even entered the room.

On the other side of the glass it was completely silent, but Nanny Piggins sniffed the air. She did not have to see or hear the witness to know who was dobbing her in.

'I'd know that slightly mouldy smell anywhere,' she declared. 'That's Mr Green! You dibber-dobber!! How dare you wrongly accuse me!!!'

She launched herself at the two-way mirror and put a large crack in it, even though it was bulletproof glass.

'You said she couldn't see me!' squealed Mr Green.

'Yes, but we didn't realise she'd be able to smell you,' protested the Police Sergeant.

The Police Sergeant tried to bustle Mr Green out of the police station before there could be an ugly confrontation, but he was too late. They met six burly police constables trying to restrain Nanny Piggins in the corridor.

'Right, I demand you take these cuffs off immediately,' declared Nanny Piggins. 'I shall need to get a good grip of his leg before I bite him.'

'It was her! I knew it, I knew she was trouble!' yelled Mr Green triumphantly.

'Oh, Father, how could you?' asked Samantha. 'You know you will only have to look after us yourself if you have Nanny Piggins arrested.'

That wiped the smile off his face.

'I'm only dobbing her in because it is the truth,' Mr Green complained petulantly.

'Sir,' chided the Police Sergeant.

'And because of the $20,000 reward,' added Mr Green, 'but it was her I saw running out of the museum at two o'clock in the morning.'

'But what were *you* doing outside the museum at 2 am?' Derrick asked.

'That's none of your business,' said Mr Green.

'You were trying to avoid going home, weren't

you?' accused Nanny Piggins. 'Monday night is the night they wax the floors in your office and you were just walking the streets until you'd be allowed back in.'

'It's not a crime that I love my job,' sniped Mr Green.

'You don't love your job,' accused Nanny Piggins. 'You just love sitting in a room where someone else pays the electricity bills!'

Mr Green was eventually escorted from the building and taken home, with only a few small bite marks on his leg. Not that Nanny Piggins had a chance to bite him. It was Michael who'd had a go, when he saw his nanny was not able to reach.

'What are we going to do?' said Samantha as they all sat in Nanny Piggins' cell, keeping her company. (The Police Sergeant was very good about letting Nanny Piggins bend the police station rules. He quite enjoyed it on the many occasions when she had been under arrest. Nanny Piggins was a lot more fun than the drunks, petty thieves and junior police officers he usually had to spend time with.)

'Everything will be all right,' said Nanny Piggins. 'If your father's evidence is all they've got against me, I'm in the clear.'

'But he's prepared to testify in court,' said Derrick.

'Yes, but the jury will soon see he's a sneaking weasel,' explained Nanny Piggins. 'Even if they believe him they'll let me off just to spite him. It's human nature.'

'Are you sure?' asked Michael.

'Absolutely,' said Nanny Piggins, 'as long as the police don't find any more evidence, I'll be fine.'

But at that very moment a constable burst into the police station brandishing a tape. 'We've got the surveillance footage!'

'Oh dear,' said Boris.

Samantha started to hyperventilate.

'What's he talking about?' demanded Nanny Piggins. 'A surveillance tape of what?'

'Let's see,' said the Police Sergeant, putting the tape in the VCR. A grainy black and white picture of the front of the museum appeared on the screen.

'There's father!' exclaimed Michael, pointing at the picture. They could see Mr Green out the front of the museum. He was on his hands and knees, with his sleeves rolled up, trying to fish change out of the museum's fountain.

'Tsk tsk tsk,' said the Police Sergeant, shaking his head. 'Constable, make a note. This afternoon we must find time to arrest Mr Green for attempting to steal small change from a charity again.'

They all turned their attention back to the screen, which was a good thing because it suddenly exploded into action. The front door of the museum burst open. The alarm siren started sounding. Mr Green was so startled he flinched forward and fell into the fountain. And an incredibly glamorous pig, with a neat little bob haircut and a black beanie jauntily perched on top of her head – ran down the front steps of the museum.

Everyone turned and looked at Nanny Piggins.

'All right, so she looks a little like me,' conceded Nanny Piggins, 'but you can't prove she took the diamond.'

Unfortunately, Nanny Piggins was immediately contradicted by the video evidence when the pig on screen paused at the bottom of the museum steps, opened her handbag, took out an enormous diamond the size of a coffee cup, looked at it, put it back in the bag, and then ran off down the street.

The children did not know what to say. They

wanted to exclaim, 'That was you!' but they did not want their words to be taken down and used as evidence against their nanny.

'How do you explain that then, Nanny Piggins?' asked the Police Sergeant. 'You say you were in your neighbour's attic. And yet there you are running out of the museum holding the Giant Mumbai Diamond.'

'Serg!' called another young constable, running over with a sheet of paper. 'The lab has just faxed through the results of the trotter-print analysis.'

The Police Sergeant took the fax and read it. 'I'm afraid the prints at the scene are an exact match to yours, Nanny Piggins.'

'Please say it wasn't you,' pleaded Samantha.

'Or it was you, but you had to do it because you were being blackmailed by someone really wicked,' pleaded Michael.

Nanny Piggins was still glaring at the frozen image of herself on the screen. 'There is a third option. It just so happens that I do know of a pig who both looks exactly like me and is a master thief.'

'You do?' said the Police Sergeant.

'Yes, my identical twin sister – Anthea Piggins!' declared Nanny Piggins.

Everyone gasped.

'Of course,' said Derrick. 'One of your identical fourteenuplet sisters!'

'It is sad that so many of your identical twin sisters don't share your strong sense of morality and public duty,' said Boris, shaking his head.

'I know,' agreed Nanny Piggins, 'but mother was not big on morality. Except when it came to food. She had very strict principles about that.'

'So you're saying that even though the pig in the surveillance footage looks exactly like you, acts exactly like you and has your exact same trotter print – that it isn't you?' asked the Police Sergeant.

'Exactly,' confirmed Nanny Piggins.

'And you expect me to believe that?' enquired the Police Sergeant.

'Well, I had assumed,' said Nanny Piggins, 'that you would be too much of a gentleman to call a lady a liar.'

'All right, then assuming I believe in this criminal doppelganger, how do you intend to prove it?' asked the Police Sergeant.

'By catching her, of course,' said Nanny Piggins.

'I don't think I can get three divisions' worth of squad cars and the sniper unit back today to track down another Piggins,' said the Police Sergeant.

'Oh, there's no need for that,' said Nanny Piggins. 'I know exactly where to find her. And if you take me along I will use my superior athletic skills to arrest her myself.'

'You're going to bite her on the leg, aren't you?' said Michael.

'Of course I am,' said Nanny Piggins. 'Coming to my home town and framing me for grand theft is inexcusable. My sisters can be very rude sometimes.'

'Surely if she has the skills of a master thief,' said the Police Sergeant, 'she would have the sense to stay hidden for a while.'

'You would think so,' agreed Nanny Piggins, 'but my sister Anthea has one great weakness.'

'Kryptonite?' guessed Michael.

'Silver bullets?' guessed Derrick.

'She can't read?' guessed Samantha.

'No,' said Nanny Piggins. 'Her great weakness is her overwhelming devotion to apricot danishes!'

'We're going to catch her because she likes apricot danishes?' asked the Police Sergeant sceptically.

'No, we're going to catch her because she *loves* apricot danishes,' corrected Nanny Piggins. 'She thinks about them, she dreams about them and, most importantly, she is physically unable to stay away from them.'

'I still don't see how that's going to help us,' said the Police Sergeant.

'It's easy,' explained Nanny Piggins. 'We will find Anthea wherever you can find the very finest apricot danish.'

'Hans' Bakery!' exclaimed the children. (All his baked products were good, but his apricot danish had just won the 'Danish by a non-Danish resident' category at the International Pastry Slamdown earlier that month.)

'Exactly!' said Nanny Piggins. 'If I know my sister, she'll be at the bakery scoffing an apricot danish as we speak.'

'Constable, get the squad car,' ordered the Police Sergeant as he leapt into action. 'We've got a lady pig to arrest! Another one!'

A short time later, the squad car pulled up outside Hans' Bakery with the Police Sergeant, the Police Constable, Nanny Piggins and the children all squashed inside. (Boris jogged along behind, because the Police Sergeant did not have a sunroof, and he would not agree to letting Boris give him one by ripping a hole in the top of his car with his bare hands.) When they peered in through Hans' shop window they could see a customer sitting at a table, eating a huge stack of danishes.

'That's her!' declared Nanny Piggins.

'It can't be,' protested Boris. 'She's a he. Look at that big bushy moustache.'

'I know that person looks nothing like me now,' said Nanny Piggins, 'but I suspect, from the natty little designer dress and perfectly coiffured bob, that he may actually be a she. And that the moustache may be a disguise.'

'No!' gasped Boris.

'You Pigginses are very good at transforming yourselves,' said Derrick.

'It is a skill you have to learn,' admitted Nanny Piggins, 'when you've been banned from as many all-you-can-eat restaurants as we have.'

'Now you've pointed it out, it is obvious she is a Piggins,' admitted the Police Sergeant. 'Just look at the way she eats those danishes.'

They watched Anthea Piggins. She was happily waggling her crossed trotters as she munched her way through six danishes at a time.

'Doesn't she ever mix it up with a cake or a meringue?' asked Michael.

'No,' said Nanny Piggins. 'It all goes back to when she was a baby and mother accidentally dropped her in a vat of apricot jam. Mother didn't notice what she had done, so Anthea had to eat her way out. She's had a passion for apricots ever since.'

'Okay, so how do you want to handle this arrest?' asked the Police Sergeant. 'I've got some tear gas in my car.'

'Good to know,' said Nanny Piggins, 'but I suppose I had better say hello before you start gassing her and I start biting her leg – she is my sister after all.'

Nanny Piggins started walking towards the shop door, but then turned and gave one more piece of advice. 'You can all come with me, but stand well back. Anthea is a master pickpocket. I suggest you keep a firm grip on your personal possessions.'

When they entered the bakery Anthea did not even notice they were there, her attention was so fully absorbed in the danishes before her.

'Hans,' said Nanny Piggins to her favourite baker as he stood behind the counter, nervous to be in the same shop as two police officers and an exact clone of his most intimidating customer. 'This is my sister,

Anthea.' Nanny Piggins pointed to her moustache-wearing identical twin. 'I want you to cut her off. No more danishes for her.'

Anthea's head snapped up. 'What–what–what?!' she exclaimed.

'But she's a good customer,' protested Hans. 'She's had nine dozen danishes in the last half hour.'

Nanny Piggins glared at Hans. 'Who is the better customer?' she asked.

'You are, Nanny Piggins, you are,' admitted Hans humbly, looking down at his shoes. He knew he should be grateful for the day Nanny Piggins moved into his neighbourhood and single-handedly quadrupled the turnover of his business.

'Sarah?!' exclaimed Anthea. 'Why would you cut me off? What have I ever done to you?'

'Impersonate me and steal a rare and famous jewel worth squillions and squillions of dollars,' answered Nanny Piggins.

'Oh yes, that,' said Anthea, taking off her fake moustache.

Everyone gasped. It was shocking how exactly she looked like Nanny Piggins. If it were not for the fact that Anthea was a blonde, whereas Nanny Piggins was a brunette, you would never be able to tell them apart.

'I'll admit that was a little naughty,' conceded Anthea, 'but I never expected it to get so out of hand.'

'Miss Piggins,' said the Police Sergeant, taking a step towards Anthea.

'You shouldn't have done that, Police Sergeant,' said Nanny Piggins. 'Anthea, give the sergeant his wallet back.'

'Sorry,' said Anthea, taking the Police Sergeant's wallet out from under a danish and handing it to Nanny Piggins. 'It's a reflex. I can't help myself.'

'How did you do that?' asked the baffled Police Sergeant. 'I didn't see you move.'

'She took it out of your pocket when you glanced at the coffee cream scroll,' explained Nanny Piggins. 'Don't worry, I'm sure Hans will sell you one before we leave. But try not to glance at it again unless you want my sister to get the packet of jelly babies in your left breast pocket.'

'Okay,' said the Police Sergeant. 'Anthea Piggins, I am arresting you for grand theft. You'd better hand over the Giant Mumbai Diamond now.'

'I can't give it to you,' said Anthea.

'Because you've sold it already and that's how you can afford all these danishes?' guessed Nanny Piggins.

'No, I bought all these danishes with cash I found in Hans' back pocket,' said Anthea.

'Hey!' said Hans, clutching his bottom and realising she was right.

'Then where's the diamond?' demanded the Police Sergeant.

'I gave it back,' said Anthea.

'To the citizens of Mumbai, because you wanted to make a political statement about the oppressive nature of colonial rule?' guessed Derrick. (He had been studying the effects of colonialism on the sub-continent in history.)

'No,' said Anthea. 'I gave it back to the man who runs the museum because that's what I was paid to do. You see, I'm a security expert now. It's what I do for a living. I test security systems to find their faults. In this instance I found if you lubricated the museum's alarm with apricot jam, the security shutters wouldn't have enough traction to close, and I'd be able to make it out of the building. But afterwards I took the diamond straight around to the curator's office and gave it to him. That was the job.'

'But he didn't say anything about that in his police statement,' protested the Police Sergeant.

'I know,' agreed Anthea, shoving another three

danishes in her mouth. 'I'm beginning to suspect that he might be a bad man.'

'There's no doubt about that,' agreed Nanny Piggins. 'Why else would he run a museum? Nasty, boring, dusty smelling places, whose sole purpose seems to be boring poor unfortunate children into a stupor.'

'Let's go and talk to him,' said the Police Sergeant.

And so they all crammed into the now even squashier squad car and drove down to the Natural History Museum. Thanks to the Police Sergeant's practised ability at bullying secretaries, they were soon ushered into the curator's office. It was a large room, lined with bookcases full of leather-bound volumes and glass display cases showing specimens from the museum's collection. The curator got up from his desk to meet them.

'Good morning, this is quite a surprise,' said the curator. He was a small neatly dressed man in his sixties. His eyes almost twinkled he seemed so delighted to be confronted by such a large group of people. 'Can I offer you anything? A slice of cake, perhaps?'

'What sort?' asked Nanny Piggins, sniffing in the general direction of the large brown cake sitting on his desk.

'Carrot cake. I made it myself,' said the curator.

'Yuck!' exclaimed Nanny Piggins. 'You'll have to come up with something better than that if you want to distract us while you leap out the window and make a run for it.'

'What are you talking about?' asked the curator, with just a little bit too much amused innocence.

'This pig –' began the Police Sergeant.

'Ahem,' interrupted Anthea and Nanny Piggins, pointedly clearing their throats.

'I mean, this lovely young lady . . . ' corrected the Police Sergeant gallantly.

Nanny Piggins and Anthea smiled.

'. . . tells us that she stole the Giant Mumbai Diamond on your orders, and that she handed the diamond back to you,' explained the Police Sergeant.

'Really?' said the curator. 'But surely you're not going to take her word for it. The word of a pig and a thief, who I just saw take the watch off your very wrist.'

Anthea handed the Police Sergeant his watch.

'Sorry,' said Anthea. 'Would you like your garters back too?'

'What?' asked the Police Sergeant.

'The garters that hold your socks up,' explained Anthea. 'I nabbed them in the police car.'

The Police Sergeant pulled up his trouser leg to see his crumpled socks. 'Yes, please.'

'You see, she can't help herself,' continued the curator, 'whereas I am a respected pillar of the museum community.' He smirked now, he was so delighted with his own cleverness.

'Would you like me to bite him, Police Sergeant?' asked Nanny Piggins as she glowered at the curator.

'I don't think that would help get a confession,' said the Police Sergeant.

'Neither do I, but it might be fun,' said Nanny Piggins.

'And if I had stolen the diamond I'd be halfway to Venezuela by now,' added the curator, 'but I have not left this room since they first informed me of the crime.'

'Hmm,' said Nanny Piggins. 'If you haven't left this room since the robbery, and my sister, who is a perfectly honest pig in all respects that don't involve apricot danishes, says she gave you the diamond, then we can deduce that the diamond must be hidden somewhere in this room.' As Nanny Piggins mulled this over she began twirling an imaginary moustache.

'Oh no,' groaned Michael. 'Nanny Piggins has been reading detective novels again.'

'I have indeed,' declared Nanny Piggins. 'I've been reading *The Purloined Letter* by Edgar Allan Poe, so I know the best way to hide something is –' she paused for dramatic effect – 'in plain view!'

'It is?' said Boris. 'I thought the best way to hide something was to put a lampshade on it.'

'Oh yes, that is the best way to hide bears,' agreed Nanny Piggins, 'but the best place to hide anything else is out in the open. Because that is the last place anybody would ever think to look.' Nanny Piggins prowled about the office. 'And so the Giant Mumbai Diamond must be hidden . . . here! In this display of rocks!' Nanny Piggins picked up a display case and dashed it on the floor, smashing the glass to smithereens. 'Behold – the Mumbai Diamond!'

Everyone looked at the grey rocks on the floor.

'You've just smashed a priceless collection of lunar specimens,' smiled the curator.

'Well then, the diamond must be here among this display of crystals,' said Nanny Piggins, picking up a second display case and throwing that on the floor too. The crystals shattered into a thousand pieces (just as a diamond would not).

'No, that was just a case of unique Amazonian crystals,' supplied the curator. 'Our staff go to a lot of trouble to label our displays; you really should take a moment to read them.'

'But the diamond has to be here somewhere!' protested Nanny Piggins.

'You'll never find it,' chortled the curator.

'Perhaps he's hidden it somewhere traditional like a wall safe or a sock drawer,' suggested Boris.

'No, criminal masterminds never do that,' said Nanny Piggins.

'I know where it is!' yelped Samantha, more surprised than anybody by her sudden insight.

'You do?' said Nanny Piggins and the Police Sergeant.

'Think about it,' said Samantha. 'Something has happened since we came in this room. Something that is not quite right.'

Everyone thought, but nobody could work it out.

'He offered us a piece of carrot cake that *he baked himself*,' said Samantha.

Nanny Piggins was immediately electrified by the importance of this fact. 'Nobody makes carrot cake for themselves because it tastes disgusting!' She turned and glared at the curator. 'The only reason anyone would bake a carrot cake is if they wanted to torture a small child by making them eat it, or if they wanted a cake that they could be sure no-one else would ever eat.'

The curator was not smiling anymore.

'Therefore,' continued Nanny Piggins, 'the diamond is in the cake!'

Nanny Piggins launched herself at the cake. And even though she was standing on the far side of the room surrounded by broken glass, lunar rocks and shards of crystal, she still had her trotters on the cake before the curator could get there. Nanny Piggins then tore the cake apart and found among the cloggy lumps of sugar, flour, butter and grated carrot (the curator was not good at baking) the sparkling perfection of the Giant Mumbai Diamond.

'Wow!' said the children.

'It's beautiful, isn't it?' said Nanny Piggins.

'Almost as pretty as an apricot danish,' agreed Anthea Piggins, taking an apricot danish out of her pocket and biting into it.

So the curator was sent away to prison for a very long time, and Nanny Piggins and the children went home. They had been given the $20,000 reward for discovering who stole the Giant Mumbai Diamond, but Nanny Piggins let Anthea keep the money. She had racked up a lot of debt because of her crippling apricot danish habit.

'Have you been traumatised by your brush with the law?' Samantha asked her nanny.

'Not at all,' said Nanny Piggins. 'I thought it was a wonderful April Fools' Day prank.'

'But the curator didn't mean it as an April Fools' Day prank,' said Derrick.

'I know, but we must give him credit where it's due,' explained Nanny Piggins. 'He may be a rotten thief and a terrible cake baker, but if he had intended this whole debacle to be a prank, then it was definitely a jolly good one.'

CHAPTER 7

Boris the Big Bad Bear

Nanny Piggins, Boris and the children were on
their hands and knees under Mrs Simpson's azalea
bushes, looking for insects. For once they were not
hunting for bugs to put in a teacher's handbag or
to run up a rude shopkeeper's leg; their search was
purely for academic purposes. You see, Samantha
had to do a project on insects for school. And Nanny
Piggins reasoned that if a picture tells a thousand
words, then an actual jar full of live insects must be

157

a million times better than the 800-word essay the teacher had actually asked for.

They already had the common fly, a ladybird, several dozen cockroaches and a worm (Nanny Piggins refused to believe that a worm was not an insect, because it was creepy and yucky and she thought it should be even if it was not). Now they were on the lookout for something venomous. Despite Samantha's protests, Nanny Piggins insisted she should try to get bonus marks by handing in something deadly. So they were just about to uproot Mrs Simpson's prize-winning dahlias to see what they would find when they heard the sound of jaunty whistling.

'What's that?' asked Nanny Piggins.

'Someone whistling,' said Derrick.

'Hmm,' said Nanny Piggins. 'I distrust whistling. Only men do it. Women are too polite to inflict their bad taste in music on others.'

'I thought people whistled because they didn't know the words to the song,' said Samantha.

'That too,' agreed Nanny Piggins. 'And thank goodness they don't know the words. It would be unbearable to have men wandering the streets bursting into show tunes. But that's beside the point. What I want to know is, who would be whistling in the street at this hour? It's too early in the morning to be that happy.'

'Shall we have a look?' suggested Michael.

'Yes, that's a good idea,' agreed Nanny Piggins, 'but we should stay hidden just in case it's that naughty Pied Piper of Hamlin.' (Nanny Piggins had read the story of the Pied Piper with the children the night before, and it had had a big impact on her. She could not believe such a horrific tale of kidnapping and rat massacre could be considered a children's story.)

Nanny Piggins and the children followed the whistler by crawling along under the hedge. All they could see of him was his shiny shoes.

'It does not bode well that his shoes are so polished,' whispered Nanny Piggins. 'Anyone who takes that much care with their appearance must want something. It's like he's trying to hypnotise us with the glare from his footwear.'

Just then the whistler stopped and turned into the Greens' very own gateway.

'He's going to our house!' whispered Samantha, panicking.

'It *is* the Pied Piper of Hamlin!' exclaimed Nanny Piggins. 'Don't worry, children, I won't let him lead you off into a cave no matter how well he plays the flute.'

But as he strode up their front path they got a view of the man with the shiny shoes for the first time. He was wearing the distinctive red tailcoat, black top hat and oily moustache that they all instantly recognised.

'The Ringmaster!' they all gasped.

'The Ringmaster is the Pied Piper of Hamlin?' whispered Michael.

'I wouldn't be surprised,' said Nanny Piggins.

'Why is he carrying a big bunch of flowers and a huge box of chocolates?' asked Derrick.

'It's just as I suspected,' whispered Nanny Piggins. 'He must want something. Here, hold my handbag, I'm going to bite him.'

'Hang on,' said Derrick, 'shouldn't you talk to him first. He hasn't done anything wrong yet.'

'Yes, but why wait?' argued Nanny Piggins. 'We all know it's just a matter of time.'

Just then the Ringmaster turned, bent down and looked straight at them.

'Sarah Piggins, darling!' said the Ringmaster. 'Is that you covered in dirt and hiding under the hedge?'

'Maybe,' admitted Nanny Piggins.

'How wonderful to see you again,' said the Ringmaster. 'Are you going to come out? Or should I crawl under there to talk to you?'

'I suppose we'll come out,' grumbled Nanny Piggins, 'but we're very busy. We still haven't found a scorpion, so we don't have much time to talk.'

'A scorpion isn't an insect, it's an arachnid,' Samantha pointed out.

'Your teachers can talk their scientific mumbo-jumbo all they like,' said Nanny Piggins. 'As far as I'm concerned, one chitin-covered invertebrate is the same as another.'

Nanny Piggins then turned and glared beadily at the Ringmaster. The box of chocolates he was carrying was a large one.

'So why are you bringing me flowers and chocolate? What do you want?' Nanny Piggins asked, resisting the urge to just grab the chocolates and make a run for it.

'Actually, darling, these aren't for you,' said the Ringmaster.

'They aren't?' questioned Nanny Piggins. 'Then what are you doing here knocking on our door?' Suddenly Nanny Piggins recoiled in shock. 'You're not after Mr Green, are you?! Although I can't deny he would make a good freak show exhibit at the circus. People would travel for miles to see the world's most boring man sitting in a damp circus tent and being boring.'

'No no, I'm not here to see him either,' said the Ringmaster. 'Although I would certainly love to meet him. The way you describe this Mr Green sounds most intriguing.'

'Then why are you here?' demanded Nanny Piggins. 'Come on, spit it out. If you're trying to use some roundabout, reverse-psychology way of luring me back to the circus, just get on with it so I can say no and carry on with my day.'

'Rest assured, I don't want a flying pig,' said the Ringmaster disdainfully, as though this was the most ridiculous idea ever.

'You don't?' asked Nanny Piggins, taken aback.

'Goodness, no! Pigs are so out of fashion,' explained the Ringmaster. 'Everyone is concerned about calories and cholesterol these days. So the idea of airborne bacon no longer has any appeal whatsoever.'

Nanny Piggins was now secretly starting to feel a little bit hurt.

'No, these days what people want is culture, art, elegance and class,' continued the Ringmaster. 'In short, they want a ballet dancing bear!'

'Boris!' gasped the children.

'Precisely,' said the Ringmaster. 'I have come to see my dear old friend Boris.'

'Hah!' scoffed Nanny Piggins. 'He'll never go anywhere with you. You hurt his feelings when you cut his act, sold his tent and made him sleep in a puddle. He'll never forget the tyrannical way you –'

But Nanny Piggins never got to finish her sentence because at that moment, Boris himself came barrelling round the corner of the house, leapt in the air, slammed into the Ringmaster and pinned him to the ground.

'Oh my goodness, Boris is going to bite the Ringmaster!' exclaimed Samantha.

But it was not to be. Instead, Boris ripped the box of chocolates out of the Ringmaster's hands, tore open the packaging and started gobbling them right there on the lawn, *without sharing*.

'Mmmnmmmglobgolbmmm,' said Boris as he devoured the chocolates.

'Boris!' said Nanny Piggins sternly. No-one loved chocolate more than her, but as far as she was concerned having a box of chocolates and not sharing with your friends was a sin so great the offender should immediately be put in jail for cruelty to chocolate lovers.

'Sorry mmmrglog can't bbmmyum resist numnumyum,' said Boris.

Eventually when every last chocolate was gone

and the wrapping had been thoroughly licked, Boris collapsed on the ground in a state of complete gluttonous exhaustion.

'I brought you flowers too,' said the Ringmaster, holding the flowers out for Boris to see.

'No thanks, I'm full now, maybe later,' said Boris.

'How could you, Boris?' chided Nanny Piggins. 'To eat a whole box of chocolates without sharing a single one! And in front of the children!!'

'I'm sorry, Sarah,' said Boris sincerely, 'but they were chocolate honey cups and you know they're my Achilles heel.'

Nanny Piggins was horrified. She turned on the Ringmaster. 'You came here to our home with chocolate honey cups! How dare you!' yelled Nanny Piggins. 'You know he's a recovering addict.'

'I only wanted to give a gift to my dear friend because I love him so,' said the Ringmaster.

'You can stop it with your oily lies,' glowered Nanny Piggins. 'My brother is wise to your ways now. He's not going anywhere with you.'

'Yes, I will,' said Boris scrambling to his feet. 'I'd do anything for another box of chocolate honey cups.'

'Boris, get a hold of yourself,' wailed Nanny

Piggins. 'Am I going to have to fetch the stepladder so I can slap you?'

'It's all right, Sarah,' said the Ringmaster. 'I'm not a bad man.'

Nanny Piggins snorted. Even the children raised their eyebrows at the brazenness of his untruths.

'Well, not very bad,' conceded the Ringmaster. 'I only want what is best for Boris and ballet lovers everywhere. It is a terrible shame for his talent to go unwitnessed.'

'It doesn't go unwitnessed,' protested Michael. 'He teaches the preschool class down at Mrs Krinklestein's ballet school.'

'And I'm sure that is very nice,' oozed the Ringmaster, 'but if he returns to the circus with me I can guarantee he will be performing to 20,000 people a night.'

'And I'll get more chocolate honey cups, right?' asked Boris.

'Of course, anything for my favourite star,' said the Ringmaster.

'You used to say I was your favourite star,' said Nanny Piggins, trying (and failing) not to look hurt.

'But you're a retiree now, darling,' said the Ringmaster. 'It's time for a younger generation to shine.'

Michael hugged Boris' leg tightly. 'You're not really going to go with him, are you?' He did not want his favourite ten-foot-tall friend to leave.

'I don't want to,' said Boris, 'but when you have a talent like mine it is a responsibility. I owe it to ballet to dance.'

Nanny Piggins snorted. 'We all know you're just doing it for the chocolate honey cups, so why not admit it?'

'So what if I am?!' protested Boris. 'You once swam the length of Lake Michigan because you could smell someone eating a cinnamon bun on the far shore.'

Nanny Piggins and Boris glowered at each other. They did not often fight, so it was distressing for the children to see them so at odds. Nanny Piggins was better at glowering than her brother. But he was six feet taller so he had a height advantage.

'Oh dear,' said the Ringmaster. 'I hate to be the cause of family disharmony.' (That was a big fat fib.) 'Perhaps Boris and I had better just leave now. You can write him a letter to apologise when you get control of your emotions, Sarah.'

The Ringmaster took Boris by the hand and started leading him away.

'Boris, don't go!' called Samantha.

Boris hesitated. He turned and looked back.

'I've got a box of chocolate honey cups in my car,' said the Ringmaster.

And that was the last they saw of Boris. He bounded down the street towards the Ringmaster's car, scrambled in through the open window and started gobbling.

'No hard feelings I hope, Sarah,' said the Ringmaster. 'You can't be cross. He came voluntarily.'

'Just go now, before your shins feel the wrath of my teeth,' advised Nanny Piggins.

The Ringmaster turned and strolled back to his car, whistling the same jaunty tune as when he'd arrived.

As soon at the car pulled away and turned around the corner, Nanny Piggins burst into tears. 'Quick, children, fetch me some chocolate, I'm so upset.'

'Do you want us to get you some chocolate honey cups?' asked Michael.

'No, I do not!' yelled Nanny Piggins. 'I say "Pish!" to that accursed confectionary and its controlling effect on my brother.'

'But if he's just going to perform ballet, surely that's not too bad,' said Samantha. 'It really is a shame that Boris is the best ballet-dancing bear in the entire world and no-one gets to see it.'

'You don't know the Ringmaster like I do,' sobbed Nanny Piggins between bites of the chocolate bar Michael had found sewn into the hem of her skirt. 'Anything involving him never ends well.'

Nanny Piggins sulked for a full forty minutes before she had eaten enough chocolate and cake to cheer herself up again. Then she got out a pen and paper to write Boris a letter.

'What are you going to write?' asked Samantha.

'Are you going to denounce him?' asked Michael.

'You are very good at denouncing,' said Derrick. 'Do you want us to fetch the thesaurus so you can look up new names to call him?'

'No,' said Nanny Piggins. 'I am going to apologise and beg forgiveness.'

'Really?' said the children. They were surprised. Nanny Piggins was normally very good at holding grudges. There were dozens of grudges she personally had been harbouring for years. Plus all the inherited grudges passed down from her mother, grandmother and great-grandmother that the Piggins family had been carefully nursing for decades. (For further information see the Buzzy Bee Biscuits chapter in *Nanny Piggins and the Wicked Plan*.)

'I love my brother and it is my duty to protect him,' explained Nanny Piggins. 'It is not his fault that honey is delicious, and that he has no willpower. But to save him from the Ringmaster I need to be with him, which means I have to start by writing a full and frank apology.'

'But it will be a fib, won't it,' asked Michael, 'because you're not really sorry?'

'Yes, but that's all right,' said Nanny Piggins, 'because sometimes when you're not really sorry, just saying you're sorry actually makes you feel sorry. So technically it is only the idea of a fib, because once you've done it, it isn't a fib anymore.'

And while the children tried to wrap their minds around the intricacies of this logic, Nanny Piggins wrote her apology letter, to which Boris replied immediately. (Once the honey cups were not clouding his brain he felt dreadful about his behaviour and he desperately wanted to make it up to his sister.)

So they arranged for Nanny Piggins and the children to pay a visit to the circus to witness his first performance.

When Nanny Piggins and the children arrived at the circus, Boris rushed to the car to greet them.

'Thank you, thank you so much for coming,' wept Boris. 'I don't know what came over me. When I'm in the presence of chocolate honey cups I lose my mind.'

'That's all right,' said Nanny Piggins, patting her brother's paw comfortingly. 'I feel the same way about chocolate biscuits, doughnuts, lemon bonbons, chocolate éclairs, chocolate ice-cream, treacle tarts, jam tarts, peanut brittle, toffee and, of course, all types of cake.'

'Thank you for coming to support me on my opening night,' said Boris.

'You're welcome,' said Samantha.

'Although it doesn't look like you need our help,' said Derrick. 'Look at all the crowds flooding in!'

There were thousands and thousands of people pouring into the Big Top.

'There must be a lot of ballet fans in this area,' said Michael.

'I know, I'm so nervous,' said Boris. 'I'd hate to brisé when I meant to assemblé and embarrass myself in front of such a large audience.'

'Hah!' said Nanny Piggins. 'If all you did was the chicken dance it would still be an honour for them to see it performed by a ballet master such as yourself.'

Boris blushed (not that you could tell with all his brown fur).

'I'd better get back to my dressing tent and get ready,' said Boris. 'I'm doing highlights from *Swan Lake* for my first act. Will you help me with my tutu and tiara?'

'Of course,' said Nanny Piggins.

Twenty minutes later Nanny Piggins had blow-dried Boris' fur, pinned his tiara to his head and zipped him up in his best white tutu. Then, after he had used up a whole box of tissues weeping at how handsome he looked, Boris was ready to go on.

'Break a leg,' said Nanny Piggins (which is what people always say in the theatre). 'Preferably not your own' (which is what people always say at the circus).

When Boris entered the Big Top the spotlight immediately found him and the audience burst into howls, cheers, applause and whistles of delight. Boris' chest swelled with pride to be greeted by such adulation. Up ahead he could see the stage and he was a little surprised to note that it was an unusual shape – square. But Boris was a professional bear, so he was not going to let a little thing like that distract him from doing a truly beautiful ballet performance.

The Ringmaster's voice boomed out over the public address system. 'And now, weighing in at 700 kilograms! And ten feet tall! Let me introduce to you – BORIS – THE – BIG – BAD – BEAR!!!'

The crowd went wild.

Boris was a little perplexed – introductions for ballet dancers did not usually involve giving their weight. But still, he was not going to be put off. He owed it to Tchaikovsky to do the best *Swan Lake* ever. So Boris drew in a deep breath and made his entrance, skipping daintily to the stage.

At this point Boris did notice that the crowd were no longer cheering. It sounded more like jeering and some very hurtful name-calling, using words like 'sissy' and 'princess'. But Boris dismissed this as an ugly argument that must have broken out between two audience members that had nothing to do with him.

Boris clambered up onto the stage, which was not so easy. Some silly-billy had put ropes all around the platform so he had squeeze between them. But once he was in position under the lights, Boris bowed gracefully to the crowd.

There was definitely more inappropriate

name-calling now, so Boris decided to silence these rude critics with the greatest display of ballet they had ever seen. The introductory overture swelled and Boris launched into his beautiful portrayal of a swan, when suddenly he felt a bump on the back of his neck. Boris ignored it for a while, continuing with his dance, but after a few seconds the bump seemed to be strangling him. So Boris looked over his shoulder and was surprised to discover a man dressed in a blue leotard, squeezing him in a head lock.

'How rude!' said Boris.

'Do you give in?' asked the leotard-wearing man.

'I don't approve of improvised dance. Would you please get off the stage, I'm doing my *Swan Lake*,' said Boris, politely but firmly.

'I'm tagging out!' said the blue leotard-wearing man as he turned and slapped the hand of a man wearing a red leotard. Now the red man sprang into the ring, climbed up on the ropes and threw himself at Boris, knocking him over.

'You're supposed to throw roses, not yourself, when you enjoy a ballet,' scolded Boris.

Fortunately Nanny Piggins was quicker on the uptake than her brother. From her position in the entry way she had seen everything and she was outraged.

'I knew it!' exclaimed Nanny Piggins. 'The Ringmaster is not interested in ballet at all. He has tricked Boris into becoming a professional wrestler!'

'No!' gasped Derrick.

'Cool!' exclaimed Michael.

'Surely that isn't fair on the other wrestlers,' worried Samantha. 'Boris is a bear and a lot bigger than a human.'

'Yes, but his heart is as soft as a marshmallow,' said Nanny Piggins.

And the children had to concede that this was true. Many was the time they had seen Boris rescue a fly and release it outside, or usher a door-to-door salesman away before Nanny Piggins could come to the front door and bite him.

'Fortunately I'm not such a soft touch,' said Nanny Piggins. 'Here, hold my handbag and my chocolate bars. No-one puts my brother in a stranglehold, crushing his best tutu, and gets away with it.'

'What are you going to do?' asked Derrick.

'Just watch,' said Nanny Piggins. She then ran full tilt at the wrestling ring, screaming her most terrifying 'HIIIIIIYYYYAAAAHHHHH!!!' When she got there Nanny Piggins bounded up onto the top of the corner post, turned and angrily shook her fist at the crowd (which only made them go wild with delight), then leapt off the post onto one of Boris' opponents.

What followed was spectacular. You would never think that a four-foot-tall pig could lift a fully grown man above her head, spin him round three times and then throw him over the ropes onto a stack of folding chairs. But that is exactly what Nanny Piggins did.

Naturally this scared his wrestling partner and he tried to run away. Unfortunately when he turned to flee he ran smack bang into Boris. And lying flat on your back on the mat is not the best defensive position when you are under attack from an angry flying pig. Nanny Piggins launched herself onto him, twisted his arms and legs into positions in which the human anatomy is never meant to be twisted, pinning his shoulders against the canvas so that he was counted out by the referee.

In the wings, the Ringmaster was horrified to see his two best wrestlers so easily dispatched and just twenty seconds into the bout. The crowd would get angry if the show stopped now. So the Ringmaster sent in another four wrestlers to take on Nanny Piggins.

Unfortunately for the Ringmaster, Nanny Piggins dealt with them with the same ease. The first one she folded up in the elasticated ropes, got Boris to pull him back, then catapulted him into the thirtieth row of the crowd. The next wrestler was a big fellow. He was almost as tall and definitely as heavy as Boris, but he had never studied the ancient art of Hapkido, so Nanny Piggins soon had him in a wristlock so painful that he was on his knees, begging to be allowed to go home. The final two wrestlers were the easiest to finish off. Nanny Piggins simply taunted them until they were quivering with rage and then, when they both launched themselves at her, she stepped out of the way so that they banged their heads together and were knocked out cold. (It is amazing the self-defence techniques you can pick up watching early morning cartoons.)

The referee then grabbed Boris and Nanny Piggins' hands, holding them high in the air.

'We have a winner!' cried the referee. 'Boris the Big Bad Bear and Nanny Piggins the World's Greatest Flying Pig!'

'Now do I get to do my ballet?' Boris asked his sister.

'I'll explain it to you when we get back to the

dressing room,' said Nanny Piggins, giving her brother's hand a reassuring squeeze.

'I was just in a wrestling match?!' asked Boris.

'Yes, but don't worry,' said Nanny Piggins. 'I will punish the Ringmaster thoroughly when I get hold of him.'

'I've never done anything tough before,' said Boris proudly. 'Wait til my friends back at the ballet company hear about this. There'll be no more taking my lunch money now.'

'Boris, you can't be happy that the Ringmaster tricked you into becoming a professional wrestler,' said Samantha.

'Well, I'll admit I'd never choose to wrestle,' agreed Boris, 'but having just been in a wrestling match without realising it, it wasn't too bad.'

Just then the Ringmaster burst into the dressing tent. (Well, actually, it is hard to 'burst' into a tent because the doors don't slam about the way they do in a proper building, but he definitely 'flapped' into the dressing tent.)

'Sarah Piggins,' denounced the Ringmaster, 'I am very cross with you.'

'How dare you!' protested Nanny Piggins. 'It is my turn to be cross with you. You're the one who tricked my brother into inadvertently taking up a dangerous extreme sport.'

'But that's nothing,' said the Ringmaster, waving the thought away. 'That's the type of thing I do all the time. You expect it when I turn up, whereas you have betrayed me by ruining my fledgling business empire.'

'What on earth are you talking about?' said Nanny Piggins.

'I have a 20,000 strong crowd out there who have all paid top dollar for tickets to see an evening of death-defying wrestling,' said the Ringmaster.

'So?' said Nanny Piggins.

'You have just broken all my best wrestlers!' complained the Ringmaster. 'The bearded lady has had to drive them to the hospital in a minibus. Half of them are too injured to ever wrestle again. And the other half are too scared of pigs to ever eat ham again.'

'It's not my fault they're so delicate,' pouted Nanny Piggins.

'This is why I tricked Boris into coming back and not you,' accused the Ringmaster. 'I knew you could not be trusted to refrain from injuring everybody.'

'It's not my fault I'm so brilliant at wrestling,' sulked Nanny Piggins.

'Someone has to go on or there will be a riot,' protested the Ringmaster.

'Well you'd better take your hat off and roll up your sleeves,' said Nanny Piggins.

'I can't wrestle!' said the Ringmaster. 'I'm in management. It would be unseemly if I let a member of staff crush my diaphragm between his thighs. How would I be able to look my trapeze artists in the eye with dignity and tell them I had just sold their net to a Japanese fisherman?'

'Yoohoo,' interrupted Boris, waving his hand and bouncing up and down in his seat like a school child. 'I don't mind going on again. I managed to get in a few pirouettes and a grand jeté while Sarah was wrestling, but I never got to do *Swan Lake* properly.'

'That crowd don't want to see ballet,' dismissed the Ringmaster. 'They're here to see violence.'

'But there's lots of violence in *Swan Lake*,' protested Boris. 'There's gun play, wickedness and drownings.'

'You might as well let Boris go on,' said Samantha. 'You don't have any choice.'

'Unless,' said the Ringmaster, turning to smile

at Nanny Piggins, 'my favourite flying pig wanted to resurrect her circus career. I have your cannon all ready.'

'I thought you said I was an old, retired has-been,' accused Nanny Piggins.

'I meant it in the nicest possible way,' smiled the Ringmaster.

'I refuse to go on anyway,' said Nanny Piggins. 'I've already damaged my dress by wrestling with all those sweaty men. I am not climbing into a cannon as well. My dry-cleaner would never forgive me. This is cashmere.'

'Then I suppose I will have to let the bear dance,' conceded the Ringmaster.

'Oh goody,' said Boris. 'This is going to be fun.'

They all watched as Boris skipped excitedly back towards the stage.

'I suppose I better introduce him,' said the Ring-master glumly, trudging after Boris.

'Do you think Boris is going to be all right?' asked Michael worriedly.

'The crowd won't tear him limb from limb, will they?' asked Samantha.

'Of course not,' said Nanny Piggins. 'You should have faith in Boris. Listen to the crowd.'

The children listened.

'I can't hear anything except Tchaikovsky music,' said Derrick.

'Exactly,' said Nanny Piggins.

When they went into the Big Top, the children were amazed to see the whole crowd enjoying Boris' beautiful ballet. You see, after watching an elegantly dressed pig perform shocking acts of brutality, the crowd found it surprisingly refreshing to see a great big bear daintily enacting a beautiful love story. (Especially when Nanny Piggins and the Ringmaster began wrestling in the background as they argued over Boris' fee. They soon came to terms after Nanny Piggins grabbed hold of the Ringmaster's moustache and swung him about in circles until he was sick.)

And so later that night, when Nanny Piggins drove Boris and the children home in Mr Green's Rolls Royce, everyone was feeling very pleased with themselves. Nanny Piggins was happy because she had put the Ringmaster in his place. Boris was happy because he'd had a lovely standing ovation from the crowd. And the children were happy because they had seen some truly spectacular wrestling moves, which they could not wait to try out on their school friends on Monday.

CHAPTER 8

Nanny Piggins: Steel Chef

Nanny Piggins, Boris and the children had spent a lovely morning playing with Samson and Margaret Wallace. Nanny Piggins was always good at thinking up activities to ensure an exciting play date, but on this particular day she outdid herself.

'We're going into town to make a mudslide,' announced Nanny Piggins.

Naturally this alarmed the children.

'But won't it destroy people's homes?' protested Derrick.

'And endanger lives?' worried Samantha.

'Of course not,' said Nanny Piggins. 'At least I don't think so, certainly not very much.'

But it turns out the children need not have worried, because Nanny Piggins had a very creative idea about how to make her own mudslide.

She took Boris and the children to the town's newly opened Water Fun Park. Then they all carried sacks full of as much dirt as they could lift (which was quite a bit, particularly in Boris' case) up to the top of the tallest water slide, threw the dirt into the swirling water and jumped in after it. The result was marvellous. It combined all the fun of a water slide, with all the joy of getting unspeakably dirty.

As luck would have it the slack-jawed teenager in charge of monitoring the ride was so lazy he did not notice that the water slide had been transformed into a mud chute until Nanny Piggins, Boris and the children had been down it five times. Then they went down it another two times while he and the rest of the fun park's staff tried to catch Nanny Piggins. (It was foolish to even try.) But luckily for them, at this point Nanny Piggins got hungry so they all left voluntarily.

The manager of the Water Fun Park did come out to scream at them about vandalising valuable equipment. But Nanny Piggins soon put him in his place, telling him that a mudslide is ten times more fun than a water slide, and if they marketed it as a 'Mud Fun Park' they would have even more customers (which, incidentally, turned out to be true. The manager was essentially a lazy man and he thought it would be easier to just change the sign at the entrance than to clean out the water slide).

So Nanny Piggins was just cleaning up Samson and Margaret by blasting them with a hose as they stood up against Mr Green's garage door, when their nanny (and Nanny Piggins' arch nemesis), Nanny Anne, appeared five minutes early, catching Nanny Piggins unaware.

'What happened to the children?' cried Nanny Anne. She hated dirt in all its forms, but she particularly hated dirt in such large quantities.

'They um . . . tripped,' suggested Nanny Piggins, 'repeatedly. In especially muddy places.'

Nanny Anne glared at Nanny Piggins. She quivered for a moment as though she was thinking up incredibly mean things to say, but then the most amazing thing happened. Instead of giving Nanny Piggins a long and boring lecture about how to be a proper nanny, Nanny Anne took a deep breath and said, 'And how are you today, Nanny Piggins?'

Everyone froze.

'What's going on?!' demanded Nanny Piggins, suddenly alarmed. 'Am I on a hidden camera TV show? Have you hired an assassin to come and get me? Have you been told by a doctor that I only have two weeks to live? Why on earth would you suddenly be nice to me?'

'She only asked how you were,' observed Derrick.

'But she's never done that before,' protested Nanny Piggins. 'Not unless she followed it up with a comment like, "Haven't you been sleeping, you've got such huge bags under your eyes?" or "You're looking a bit green. Are you unwell, or is it just the colour of your dress that does that to you?"'

'Ha, ha, ha,' said Nanny Anne, mimicking the noise of normal human laughter. 'Oh, Nanny Piggins, you are such an adorable character.'

'You're right! She does want something!' exclaimed Michael.

'Either that or she has been kidnapped by aliens and this is a Nanny Anne clone,' said Samantha, peering at Nanny Anne to see if there were any protruding robot parts.

Nanny Piggins stood protectively in front of the children.

'Stop trying to be nice, you're not very good at it, and you're frightening the children,' demanded Nanny Piggins. 'Just tell us what you want.'

'Oh, all right,' said Nanny Anne. 'The *Steel Chef* Show is coming to town.'

'Oooh, I love that show,' said Boris excitedly. 'The Steel Chef is so rude.'

'They are looking for cooking contestants,' continued Nanny Anne. 'If you and I team up, with your flare for desserts, and my ability to actually follow a recipe – we'd be unstoppable.'

'I don't want to team up with you!' said Nanny Piggins. 'I'd sooner cook with a baboon.' She turned to the children and explained, 'Baboons are very good at making sauces. They've got tremendous patience with the stirring.'

'Well, too bad. You don't have any choice,' said Nanny Anne, 'because I've already put our names down and you can't change teams once you've entered.'

'Why on earth did you do that?' protested Nanny Piggins.

'I didn't want you teaming up with someone else against me,' explained Nanny Anne. 'Now all that's decided, I'd better take Samson and Margaret home to wash them properly. I'll see you tomorrow morning for the tryouts.'

They watched as Nanny Anne lead her two soggy charges away.

'What are you going to do?' asked Derrick

'Isn't it obvious?' asked Nanny Piggins.

'Chase after Nanny Anne and bite her for her impertinence?' asked Michael.

'No,' said Nanny Piggins, 'although that is a good idea. But I have decided I will go along with Nanny Anne's scheme.'

'Really?!' exclaimed Samantha.

They were all surprised.

'It is true that I cannot stand Nanny Anne,' admitted Nanny Piggins, 'and it takes all my strength of will not to pick up a handful of mud and rub it in her hair every time I see her. Still, it would not be fair to the television viewers of the world to deny them the opportunity to see me cook. Therefore, I shall compete.'

The next day Nanny Piggins, Boris and the children arrived at the local football stadium. So many people were trying out it was the only place in town that would hold them all. It was quite a sight to behold. Five hundred trestle tables with camping stoves and portable ovens all set up for one thousand would-be Steel Chefs.

They found Nanny Anne at the first trestle table in the front row. (She had secured it by arriving at 3 am, four hours before anyone else.) She was just arranging all her equipment on her half of the table, using a set square and protractor so everything was perfectly at right angles, when Nanny Piggins emptied out her own box of equipment.

'Is that all you brought?' asked Nanny Anne, looking at Nanny Piggins' well worn collection of bowls, spoons and saucepans.

'I don't need anything else,' said Nanny Piggins dismissively.

'What about scales?' asked Nanny Anne.

'I don't believe in measuring things when I cook,' said Nanny Piggins. 'It takes the surprise out of the final result.'

'What about your food processor?' asked Nanny Anne.

'I never use one,' said Nanny Piggins. 'Too much washing up.'

'Where's your colander?' asked Nanny Anne.

'Oh, we lost that weeks ago when we were catching tadpoles in a stormwater drain,' said Nanny Piggins. 'But don't worry. I did bring our remaining badminton racquet. I can strain pasta with that.'

'I can see I am going to have to do everything myself,' said Nanny Anne, which she was secretly glad about. She was not a woman who enjoyed delegating (or anything really, except disapproving of people).

'Where are Sampson and Margaret today?' asked Nanny Piggins.

Nanny Anne momentarily looked confused, as if she did not know who Nanny Piggins was talking about. But she never got to answer because just then a microphone crackled and a harassed-looking producer addressed the assembled crowd.

'Thank you all for coming,' said the producer. 'The first sudden death elimination round will begin in a few minutes. But before we start, let's have some inspiring words from the Steel Chef himself . . . Mr Kimuzukashii!'

Mr Kimuzukashii strode out onto the stage. He was a short but very angry-looking Japanese man with Elvis-style hair, dressed in a colourful silk dressing-gown, cravat and cowboy boots.

The crowd broke into rapturous applause. Some

more hysterical *Steel Chef* fans screamed like pop groupies, then fainted (which is not a smart thing to do when there are lots of sharp cooking implements around).

Mr Kimuzukashii stood in front of the microphone, glared angrily at the crowd, then commenced screaming at them in a torrent of Japanese.

'What's he saying?' asked Michael.

'I don't know,' admitted Nanny Piggins, 'but it doesn't sound very friendly, does it? I speak some Japanese, but he's using words which I think are too rude to be included in the standard Berlitz phrasebook.'

Fortunately a translator appeared and spoke into a second microphone.

'I have no doubt you are all terrible cooks,' interpreted the translator calmly. Everyone in the audience cheered. The Steel Chef was famous for his rudeness.

'I am just grateful that I do not have to soil my mouth with any of the food you prepare here today. Fortunately my team of minions will take care of that. I doubt any of you are really worthy of competing against me. It disgusts me to look at you, let alone eat your food,' concluded Mr Kimuzukashii, before stalking off the stage.

'Isn't he dreamy?' sighed Nanny Anne.

'He needs a short sharp bite to the shin if you ask me,' scowled Nanny Piggins.

'All right then,' said the producer, returning to the microphone, 'we commence cooking in sixty seconds. The rules are simple. One – you must make an entree, main course and dessert. Two – you must not interfere with or even touch another competitor's food or utensils. And three – you must use the Steel Chef's special ingredient, which is . . .' a stagehand wheeled out a trolley and whipped off a stainless steel cover to reveal a huge plate of pale, slimey stuff. 'Tofu!'

'Yes!' cried Nanny Anne, pumping her fist in the air. She was glad she had stayed up last night memorising her tofu cookbook now.

Nanny Piggins glowered. 'Is this some kind of trick? I don't believe tofu really is a food. It looks disgusting, if feels disgusting and it tastes disgusting. Why is tofu a food and dirt isn't? At least dirt is a nice chocolatey brown colour.'

'You have thirty minutes, beginning now!' said the producer, starting a giant stopwatch.

'I'll take care of the entree and main. Can I trust you to handle the dessert?' asked Nanny Anne.

'Fine,' muttered Nanny Piggins.

Nanny Anne frantically set to work. She had

been maniacally beating, chopping, steaming and seasoning for fifteen minutes before she looked round to see what Nanny Piggins was up to. And she was horrified to discover the answer was – nothing.

Nanny Piggins was sitting on the ground, her head clutched in her trotters, rocking back and forth.

'What's she doing?!' screeched Nanny Anne.

'Thinking,' explained Derrick.

'But she's supposed to be cooking,' shrieked Nanny Anne, her voice getting higher with every syllable.

'I think she's trying to figure out how to make something as disgusting as tofu into something as delicious as a dessert,' explained Samantha.

'Nanny Piggins doesn't know any tofu recipes,' added Michael.

'Terrific, so I'm going to have to cook the dessert as well!' said Nanny Anne. 'When we get home, *someone* is going to spend a lot of time sitting on the naughty step.'

But that was not to be, because just then Nanny Piggins startled them all by leaping to her trotters and yelling, 'I've got it! Stand back!'

Nanny Piggins then launched into cooking in much the same way she used to be launched out of a cannon. She moved in such a blur of speed it was impossible to see what she was doing.

'Only two minutes to go,' said Nanny Anne nervously. She had finished both her courses with three minutes to spare, because she wanted to touch up her hair and make-up before the judges came around.

The clock ticked on mercilessly. Pretty soon Nanny Piggins only had ten seconds to go and her flurry of activity had not slowed or showed any sign of producing a result. The children watched the seconds tick away. They did not like to count down, in case it made their nanny nervous and she started biting people.

When the last second ticked by, the producer took the microphone. 'Step away from your utensils.'

All the would-be cooks stepped back. (Except a few who collapsed sobbing on the floor, or over their failed plates of congealed tofu.)

'Finished!' announced Nanny Piggins, stepping back from her giant pot.

The judge came to Nanny Piggins and Nanny Anne's table first.

'Let's see,' said the judge. She sniffed Nanny Anne's entree, 'Braised tofu with vegetables? Very nice.' She put a big tick on her notepad. She then took a small taste of Nanny Anne's main course, 'Salt and pepper tofu? Mmm, tasty.' Another big tick. 'And what's this?' asked the judge, pointing at Nanny Piggins' cooking pot.

'Prepare to taste the finest dessert ever made from tofu!' announced Nanny Piggins, before whipping off the lid.

The judge, Nanny Anne and the children peered into Nanny Piggins' cooking pot. It contained an enormous volume of brown liquid.

'It looks like chocolate pudding,' said the judge.

'It is chocolate pudding,' said Nanny Piggins proudly. 'Try some.'

The judge picked up a teaspoon, scooped out a small morsel and tasted it. 'Mmmm-mm-mmm that's good,' said the judge, 'but I couldn't taste the tofu.'

'You have to dig deeper for that,' said Nanny Piggins.

'Okay,' said the judge, taking another spoonful, then another, then another, trying to get to the tofu. By the time the judge's spoon found the tofu she had eaten twenty litres of Nanny Piggins' finest chocolate pudding. 'This pudding is so good, but I don't think I can manage the tofu. I couldn't eat another bite.'

'Precisely!' exclaimed Nanny Piggins. 'Because the best way to serve tofu is under twenty litres of chocolate pudding so by the time you find the tofu, there's no way you'll be able to eat it.'

And fortunately for the two nannies, the judge was now so addled on sugar that she thought this reasoning made perfect sense. She gave Nanny Piggins fifteen ticks for her pudding (fourteen more than she should have) and they went through to the next round.

And so the day progressed. Nanny Anne conscientiously made healthy entrees and mains, while Nanny Piggins transformed weird and disgusting ingredients into spectacular desserts. At the end of the day they had survived all the sudden-death elimination rounds to be among the six remaining teams who would compete in the televised semifinals the next day.

'Well done, Nanny Piggins!' said Samantha.

'I can't believe you're going to be on *Steel Chef*,' said Michael.

'Really?' said Nanny Piggins. 'I can't believe they haven't asked me to be on it earlier. I guess they didn't want a pig to show up all the humans for the limited cooks that they are. Let's go home.'

Nanny Piggins turned to Nanny Anne to see if she needed a lift in Mr Green's Rolls Royce (Boris had borrowed it from the car park at Mr Green's work and was coming to pick them up). And that was when they noticed for the first time that Nanny Anne had gone a sick shade of white, frozen like a statue and was muttering strange sounds to herself.

'Are you all right, Nanny Anne?' asked Michael.

'Eu-bzzaa-engh,' said Nanny Anne.

'Do you think I should slap her?' asked Nanny Piggins hopefully.

'I can't believe it,' muttered Nanny Anne. 'I'm going to be on *Steel Chef*. Mummy will be so proud.'

'She has a mother?' questioned Derrick.

'I always assumed she had hatched from a pod,' said Nanny Piggins.

'I think she's gone into shock,' said Samantha.

'Should we put a tourniquet on her arm and make her lie very still?' asked Nanny Piggins.

'That's what you do for snake bite,' said Michael.

'I know,' admitted Nanny Piggins. 'I really should finish reading that first aid book. But all the exciting things are in the first chapter. It's much more fun to learn about shark attacks and spider venom than how to treat a nosebleed. If we could just find a scorpion to bite her I'd know exactly what to do.'

'Come on, Nanny Anne, we'll take you home,' said Samantha. 'You need a good night's sleep.'

'Sleep!' shrieked Nanny Anne, suddenly snapping out of her catatonic state. 'There's no time for sleep! I'm going to be on *Steel Chef*! I have recipes to learn.' Then she took off into the night, running as fast as she could, abandoning all her kitchen equipment.

'Where do you think she's going?' asked Derrick.

'She's not heading the right way for her house,' added Michael.

'Should we go after her?' asked Samantha.

'No, she'll be all right,' said Nanny Piggins. 'A brisk jog will do her good.'

Nanny Piggins and the children headed home to enjoy a few chocolate cakes and a relaxing horror movie before turning in for the night.

They returned to the football stadium the next day, but during the night the venue had been transformed. The trestle tables were gone. Instead there were thousands of chairs set out, ready for the capacity crowd that would be descending later that night.

A huge stage had been built, and on the stage

there were three separate kitchens. Behind the kitchens were a raised platform and giant playback screen, where the Steel Chef and rude celebrity judges would sit over the contestants for the duration of the show. The format was simple – there would be two semifinals with three teams competing in each. Then the grand final where the two winners would compete head-to-head with Mr Kimuzukashii for the title of Steel Chef.

Nanny Anne and Nanny Piggins sat backstage during the first semifinal. Nanny Anne used the opportunity to chant measurement conversion tables, while Nanny Piggins played handball with the stagehands.

After what felt like eons, one of the production assistants approached them. 'I'll be leading you up on stage in two minutes,' she said.

'Oh my goodness,' said Nanny Anne. 'I'm so nervous.'

'You'll be fine,' Nanny Piggins assured her. 'The worst that can happen is that it all goes terribly wrong and you humiliate yourself in front of a crowd of 30,000 people, as well as millions of viewers at home.'

Nanny Anne now could not speak. She stared at Nanny Piggins with even greater wide-eyed panic.

'You're on,' said the assistant. 'Follow me.'

Nanny Piggins followed, dragging the now borderline hysterical Nanny Anne out onto the huge stage. They were blinded by the lights at first. But after blinking a few times, their eyes adjusted and they could make out the thousands of faces staring back at them from the darkness.

'Oh my good gracious me,' said Nanny Anne, which really is a testament to her strength of will – even though she was terrified out of her wits she still had the delicacy not to swear.

Nanny Piggins, on the other hand, thrived in front of an audience. Her chest puffed out, her snout rose proudly and she sniffed the adrenaline in the air. She was soon running back and forth across the front of the stage, leading the crowd in a Mexican wave.

'Contestants to your cooking stations!' announced the producer.

Nanny Piggins reluctantly left the adoring crowd and took her place alongside Nanny Anne.

'The show starts in . . . three, two, ONE!!!'

The crowd roared. Smoke billowed out from behind Nanny Piggins. She looked round to see Mr Kimuzukashii rising upwards on a platform with pneumatic grace. He stood proudly, scowling with his arms crossed, assuming enormous dignity for a man wearing what looked like a lady's dressing-gown.

'You compete for the right to cook against me – the Steel Chef!' he shouted angrily in Japanese, before being translated by the much calmer interpreter.

'You will prepare three dishes. And your special ingredient is . . .' he held his hand out dramatically, indicating the front of the stage.

A stagehand wheeled out a trolley, then whipped back the cover to reveal the secret ingredient.

'Bean sprouts!' screamed the Steel Chef.

'Thank goodness!' exclaimed Nanny Anne.

'Bottom!' moaned Nanny Piggins.

'Begin!' screamed the Steel Chef.

Nanny Anne launched herself into her cooking. She ran to the trolley, grabbed an armful of sprouts, ran back and immediately started sautéing, chopping and mashing.

Nanny Piggins did not move with anywhere near her speed. She was too depressed. It was hard to find joy in the opportunity to show off in front of a huge crowd when all you had to work with was bean sprouts. She wished she had brought her cannon with her, so she could at least blast the bean sprouts into the sky. That would be a lot better than eating them. Nanny Piggins was not even sure what a bean sprout was. She had heard of beans and brussels sprouts, so she assumed it was some horrible genetically modified combination.

She cautiously trudged over to the trolley and sniffed at the small thin vegetables. Then she picked one up and licked it. 'Not too bad, I suppose,' muttered Nanny Piggins. Then she put it in her mouth, but she only got in one chew before she was overwhelmed by the disgusting flavour. 'Ew, gross!' said Nanny Piggins, spitting the bean sprout on the stage. 'Pah, yuck, yucky!'

'Would you just start cooking something?!' yelled Nanny Anne, barely looking up from the grey gloop of her simmering bean sprouts.

'Mmm,' said Nanny Piggins, a smile spreading across her face. 'I know just what to do with them.' She set to work.

At the end of the half hour Nanny Anne was flushed but happy. She knew her bean sprout soup and bean sprout dumplings were equal to anything the opposition made. No-one knew how to cook with unpleasant health foods like Nanny Anne.

And Nanny Piggins seemed very proud of the concoction she was stirring carefully in her saucepan.

The dishes were carried up to the Steel Chef and rude celebrity judges. They declared Nanny Anne's soup to be 'adequate' and her dumplings 'fair, if bordering on the banal', which made Nanny Anne weep because this was high praise indeed from the Steel Chef. Then the judges turned to Nanny Piggins' dessert.

The Steel Chef yelled and screamed in Japanese for several minutes, which the translator calmly interpreted as: 'And what is this dish?'

'Chocolate fondue,' explained Nanny Piggins. 'Bean sprouts are disgusting if you chew them, but they are not so bad if you just lick them. So I thought they would make the perfect dipping ingredient for a fondue. Far better than dipping strawberries because you might be tempted to bite a strawberry, thereby ruining the purity of the chocolate experience.'

The Steel Chef glowered at Nanny Piggins. She smiled back. He picked up a bean sprout and dipped it in the fondue, then stuck it in his mouth. He sucked for a moment, took the bare bean sprout out of his mouth and looked at it, then declared, 'Oshikatta.'

The translator gasped. He had never heard the Steel Chef use this word before. 'He said, it's tasty!' stammered the translator.

Now there were gasps from the whole crowd.

'You win the honour of competing against me in the finals!' announced the Steel Chef.

'We're through to the finals!' squealed Nanny Anne. She was so happy, she briefly considered hugging Nanny Piggins. But she did not get the opportunity because Nanny Piggins was running back and forth in front of the crowd, leading Mexican waves again.

Nanny Piggins and Nanny Anne had a short break backstage before they had to go back on for the finals.

'Now, Nanny Piggins,' said Nanny Anne in her most superior, smug voice. 'This is the final. And while winning is important, not humiliating me is even more important. So I think you should let me decide the dessert this time. I doubt you will continue to get away with your stunt recipes.'

'How dare you!' said Nanny Piggins. 'I'm twice the cook you are. At least my meals bring happiness to those who eat them.'

'Happiness and type 2 diabetes!' retorted Nanny Anne. 'If it wasn't for my well balanced, traditional cooking we would not have got this far.'

'If it wasn't for my restraint in not biting your leg on one of the several thousand occasions when I have been sorely provoked, we would not have got this far,' retorted Nanny Piggins.

'Maybe I'll make an alternative dessert and let the judges decide which is best,' said Nanny Anne.

'Maybe I'll make an alternative main and entree and they won't have room for dessert,' said Nanny Piggins.

'Ladies, you're needed on stage,' interrupted a stagehand.

Nanny Anne and Nanny Piggins strode back out into the limelight. In the finals they were competing against two men who ran a fusion restaurant in the city and, of course, the Steel Chef himself.

'Hah, a bunch of men, we'll win easily,' said Nanny Piggins confidently.

They waited for the music and smoke machine to start up, but it did not. Instead the producer and Mr Kimuzukashii walked out onto the stage.

'Before we begin,' said the producer, 'there is an announcement. During the break we reviewed the footage and one contestant was caught breaking the rules.'

'What did you do?' wailed Nanny Anne, turning on Nanny Piggins.

'Nothing!' protested Nanny Piggins.

'You,' said the Steel Chef, dramatically pointing at Nanny Anne, 'were caught on camera interfering with a competitor's utensils.'

Up on the giant replay screen behind them there suddenly appeared playback footage of Nanny Anne as she snuck over to her competitor's kitchen area and put a dirty dish in a sink full of soapy water.'

'I only put them in the sink to soak so they would be easier to wash later,' protested Nanny Anne. 'I can't bear untidiness.'

'You broke the rules, you are disqualified, leave the stage immediately!' commanded the Steel Chef.

'Noooooooo!!!' cried Nanny Anne.

Two enormous sumo wrestlers came out to escort her offstage. It took them a while because Nanny Anne dodged and weaved to evade them, then hung onto the oven door with all her strength before they finally yanked her free and carried her off.

'But please, this is all I have, showing people up and proving I'm better than everyone else is what I live for!' wailed Nanny Anne. The last Nanny Piggins saw of her was her weeping face disappearing into the darkness.

'What about me?' Nanny Piggins asked the Steel Chef.

'You may continue to compete but must do so alone,' declared the Steel Chef.

'The two men in the opposing team sniggered. Even the Steel Chef was not competing alone. He had an assistant, a master chef in his own right, who would do all the chopping and stirring for him.

Nanny Piggins began to feel a rare and unfamiliar emotion – she was daunted. She looked out at the food-loving crowd. She did not want to let them down. Could she really pull this off? Three dishes in thirty minutes. She only had four trotters.

'And now it is time to reveal the special ingredient,' announced the Steel Chef. 'It is . . .'

The trolley was wheeled out.

'Chocolate!' screamed the Steel Chef.

The stagehand whipped off the cover to reveal a huge platter of delicious chocolate.

'Yes!' cried Derrick, Samantha and Michael from their seats in the audience. Boris just wept.

Up on stage, a huge smile spread across Nanny Piggins' face. She had it in the bag. No-one knew chocolate like Nanny Piggins.

What followed was the most spectacular culinary demonstration ever performed. Nanny Piggins did not just cook. She put on a show. She used the lighting grid above the stage to swing about like a trapeze artist while whipping her egg whites. She juggled a razor sharp meat cleaver and flaming blowtorch to slice her chocolate buttons and melt them in midair. And she tap danced while singing an aria from *Carmen* as she creamed her sugar and butter.

When the time elapsed, and Nanny Piggins shook the final dash of icing sugar onto her creations, the crowd rose as one to give her a standing ovation.

The judges sampled the fusion chefs' food first. They had made impressively innovative choices and the judges were admiring of their presentation, but the kindest thing they had to say about the taste of the food was that it was 'interesting'.

Next, it was the Steel Chef's turn. The celebrity judges were not rude to him at all. They had seen Mr Kimuzukashii at work with his sashimi slicer and did not want to get on his bad side. But the Steel Chef was a specialist in subtle Asian flavours. The rich and creamy taste of chocolate was not really a strength of his.

Finally it was time to judge Nanny Piggins' dishes.

'What have you made?' asked the ruder of the two celebrity judges.

'For my entree, I made a chocolate cake. For the main course, I made a chocolate cake. And for dessert, I made a chocolate cake,' announced Nanny Piggins.

The crowd gasped at her bold menu.

'But you have made three desserts, not three separate courses,' protested the less rude judge.

'When you are as good at making chocolate cake as me, it would be a crime to make anything else,' argued Nanny Piggins. 'Just try some.'

The judges each took a slice of the first cake, and tried it. Then they tried a slice of the second cake. Then the third. Then they picked up the cakes in their hands and ravenously gobbled them up, pushing and shoving each other as they tried to eat the most.

'You're right. These are the best cakes I have ever eaten,' said the very rude judge, with cake crumbs and whipped creamed smeared all over his face.

'There is one clear winner – Nanny Piggins is the new Steel Chef!!!' declared the less rude judge, with which the two sumo wrestlers brought out the coveted Steel Chef's solid steel hat and placed it on Nanny Piggins' head.

Nanny Piggins started doing triumphant laps around the stage, only occasionally having to dodge the utensils and sharp knives the old Steel Chef was throwing at her.

Later that night Nanny Piggins, Boris and the children drove home in Mr Green's Rolls Royce feeling very happy indeed.

'Oh, Nanny Piggins, we're so proud of you,' said Samantha.

'What are you going to do with your Steel Chef's hat?' asked Derrick.

'I think I will give it to Nanny Anne,' said Nanny Piggins. 'It means more to her. And without her I would not have even bothered entering, let alone getting through all those elimination rounds.'

'That's awfully nice of you,' said Michael, shocked by his nanny's uncharacteristic generosity towards her arch nemesis.

'Don't worry,' said Nanny Piggins. 'I won't do it nicely. I'll go round and throw it through her bedroom window, then run away. I haven't completely forgotten myself.

So they drove home to recreate Nanny Piggins' winning dishes in the comfort of their own kitchen, where they could gobble the cakes themselves without having to share a single bite with any rude celebrity judges.

CHAPTER 9

Nanny Piggins Saves Christmas

'T was the night before Christmas, so naturally Nanny Piggins was up on the roof Santa-proofing the house by fastening chicken wire over the chimney.

'Right, pass me the nail gun,' instructed Nanny Piggins.

'You know Santa Claus is not a bad person,' said Michael, handing it to her.

'I know that,' said Nanny Piggins.

'Thwack! Thwack! Thwack!' went the nail gun.

'No-one likes getting presents from strangers more than me,' continued Nanny Piggins, 'but that doesn't mean that breaking and entering is all right. If he wants to give us gifts he should knock on the door, come in and have a slice of cake like a normal person.'

The children looked at each other. Their nanny was not accustomed to the finer points of Christmas. Because, you see, she had lived most of her life in the circus, and the Ringmaster never let them celebrate the yuletide holiday. (In fact, he never let them celebrate any holiday. He even discouraged them from knowing the day of the week. Anything that allowed them to measure time, and realise how long they had been working for him, was strictly forbidden.)

'It amazes me that one overweight man, wearing a bright red fur-trimmed suit no less, manages to go on a worldwide crime spree on the same night every year and nobody has ever done anything about it!' said Nanny Piggins. 'You'd think at the very least the animal rights activists would have a go at him for wearing fur.'

'Perhaps they don't because they like getting presents,' suggested Michael.

'You're probably right,' agreed Nanny Piggins.

'So few people have principles anymore. Especially when it comes to a stocking full of chocolate treats and toys. Now where's my note?'

Derrick handed his nanny the note she had written earlier. It read:

Dear Mr Santa Claus,
Kindly refrain from breaking into this home via the chimney. If you were a true gentleman you would knock at the front door and introduce yourself. Or at the very least climb in through the upstairs bathroom window like a normal person.

Kind Regards

Nanny Piggins F.P. (Flying Pig)

'There, that ought to do it,' said Nanny Piggins as she used the nail gun to fix the note to the chimney stack.

Boris promptly burst into tears. Celebrating Christmas was new for him too, but unlike Nanny Piggins he was anxious not to miss out. 'But what about me?' blubbered Boris. 'My shed doesn't have a chimney. How am I going to get my presents?'

Samantha gave Boris' leg a comforting hug. 'I'm sure he'll climb in through the window or dismantle part of the roof. After all, he's Santa, so he's got lots of initiative.'

'I hope so,' said Boris, struggling to control his tears. 'It's just that I really do like getting presents.'

'It's bears like you who send mixed messages to burglars,' said Nanny Piggins sternly. 'Either it's all right to break into people's homes or it's not.'

'You break into people's homes all the time,' Derrick pointed out.

'But that's different,' protested Nanny Piggins.

'How?' asked Michael.

Fortunately Nanny Piggins was saved from having to find logic in her argument because at this point they were interrupted by a noise from below.

'There is someone on the street,' whispered Derrick.

'Is it the Police Sergeant?' asked Nanny Piggins. 'I called him and reported that there was a large fat man, wearing red, breaking into houses tonight. True, he did laugh at me and hang up. But perhaps he has decided to do something about it after all.'

They all crept to the edge of the roof and looked over. And they were startled by what they saw. It was not the Police Sergeant. No, it was someone much more impressive. It was the greatest annual home intruder of them all.

'It's Santa Claus!' gasped Nanny Piggins.

There was no mistaking the red clothes, the white beard, the sack full of toys and the 'little round belly that shook when he laughed like a bowl full of jelly' (not that he laughed while they were watching him, but he did sneeze and it definitely wobbled then).

'But where are his reindeer?' asked Boris. It did seem strange to see Santa travelling on foot. He did not look like a man who exercised regularly.

'Perhaps they've ditched him because they don't want to do jail-time,' said Nanny Piggins.

'He's got a lot of toys in that sack,' said Michael. 'I hope he's got something good for us.'

'Pass me the nail gun again,' said Nanny Piggins. 'I'll give him a present if he tries getting down our chimney.'

'You can't shoot Santa with a nail gun!' protested Samantha.

'Not even a little bit?' asked Nanny Piggins.

'No!' exclaimed the children.

'I could just nail his boots to the roof until the police get here,' suggested Nanny Piggins.

'He's got to deliver presents to all the boys and girls in the world,' explained Derrick. 'He hasn't got time to be arrested.'

'He's only got to deliver them to all the *good* boys and girls,' muttered Nanny Piggins. 'That's probably only seven or eight children on the entire planet. After all, 365 days in a row is an awfully long time to expect children to behave themselves. Most of them struggle to keep it up for five minutes. Delivering presents to *good* children will probably only take him an hour or two. Then he'll go home to the North Pole and watch television.'

'Well, I've been a good boy and I'm not letting him forget about me!' declared Boris as he leapt up to his full height, waved his arms and called out, 'Hey, Santa! I live in the shed around the back. I haven't got a chimney but I'll leave out a chainsaw and you can cut a hole in the roof if you like.'

Unfortunately Santa Claus was so shocked to suddenly be addressed by a ten-foot-tall bear standing on a rooftop, that he stumbled backwards, dropping his sack and falling into the gutter, where he hit his head hard on the edge of the pavement.

'Oh my goodness!' exclaimed Samantha. 'You've killed Santa!!!'

Boris burst into tears. 'I didn't mean to!' he sobbed.

'Don't worry, I'll first-aid him,' said Nanny Piggins. 'He may be an international master criminal, but if he needs an icepack I'm just the pig for the job!' With that dramatic statement, Nanny Piggins leapt straight off the roof.

When the children rushed to look over the edge they were relieved to discover Nanny Piggins had caught the branch of a tree. (She had been watching *Robin Hood* and had seen Errol Flynn do something very similar, so she had been secretly practising leaping out of her second-storey bedroom window all week.) She then climbed down the tree and rushed over to Santa.

The children hurried back into the attic, ran down the stairs and out through the house to help her (which only took three seconds more, but was nowhere near as impressive).

'Is he all right?' asked Derrick.

'Well, he's breathing,' said Nanny Piggins, 'but just look at him! He's wearing a red jacket with red trousers?! His dress sense is in serious trouble.'

'Maybe that's fashionable at the North Pole,' suggested Boris.

'Looking silly isn't fashionable anywhere,' said Nanny Piggins firmly, 'unless you're a clown and then it is an unfortunate occupational requirement.'

'Check his pupils,' suggested Samantha.

'His what-whats?' asked Nanny Piggins.

'The black part of his eyes,' explained Derrick.

'Why?' asked Nanny Piggins.

'That's what they always do on TV medical dramas,' explained Samantha.

'Then it must be right,' decided Nanny Piggins. She pulled up each of Santa's eyelids and had a look at his eyes. (This was easy to do because she had been eating toffee so her trotters were sticky and it was easy to get a good grip on his eyelashes.) 'Mmm,' said Nanny Piggins. 'Yep, they definitely look like eyes.'

'Shouldn't we call an ambulance?' asked Michael.

'We could,' said Nanny Piggins, 'but they would only call the police. And you know the Police Sergeant made me promise I would not make any more citizens' arrests this week.'

Nanny Piggins had tried arresting the Post Mistress at their local post office, arguing that the length of her queues were a cruel and unusual punishment, and that since torture had been outlawed under the Geneva Convention, the Post Mistress clearly should be thrown in jail.

'You don't want me to spend Christmas Day in jail, do you?' asked Nanny Piggins.

'You spent Easter in jail and you said you enjoyed it,' Derrick reminded her.

Nanny Piggins had been arrested after hurling herself at an Easter bunny in the shopping centre and wrestling him to the ground. In the end she was let off because, as she told the judge, 'The Easter bunny only had himself to blame. Dressing up in a full-sized bunny suit and handing out free chocolate is like dressing up as a zebra and standing in the lion enclosure at the zoo.'

'Yes, but I got to eat all the Easter bunny's chocolate before I was arrested,' said Nanny Piggins. 'I haven't had my Christmas lunch yet. And you promised to make the most wonderful Christmas lunch ever, so I don't want to miss that.'

'We can't leave Santa unconscious and lying on the footpath on Christmas Eve,' said Derrick. 'What are we going to do with him?'

'Isn't it obvious?!' exclaimed Nanny Piggins.

'No,' said the children.

'I may not know a lot about celebrating Christmas, but I have watched every Christmas movie and television special ever made,' said Nanny Piggins. 'So I know that when Santa falls ill, or sprains his ankle, or is kidnapped, it is the job of the first person who finds out to take over and do his job.'

'What are you saying?' asked Samantha. (Samantha actually knew exactly what Nanny

Piggins was saying, but she was desperately hoping she was wrong.)

'I shall be Santa Claus and deliver presents to all the boys and girls of the world!' declared Nanny Piggins.

'All the *good* boys and girls,' corrected Boris.

'No, I'm going to give presents to the bad children as well. Unlike Santa I believe in positive reinforcement,' explained Nanny Piggins. 'If they're behaving badly and you want them to improve, you have to use the carrot as well as the stick.'

'But you always say you'd rather be hit by a stick than have to eat a carrot,' argued Michael.

'Just because the expression doesn't make any sense doesn't make it any less true,' said Nanny Piggins sternly. 'Now help me get Santa inside.'

'Do you want me to carry him?' asked Boris.

'No, I think we'd better drag him,' said Nanny Piggins. 'He's a heavy one and I'd hate for you to get a hernia on the night before Christmas. Especially when you promised to perform the entire *Nutcracker* ballet for us after lunch tomorrow.'

And so Nanny Piggins, Boris and the children dragged Santa inside (only banging his head three times on the edge of the garden path and once on the telephone table in the hallway).

'What next?' asked Samantha. 'Are you going to put on Santa's clothes?'

'First of all,' said Nanny Piggins, 'it would be highly impertinent to undress the man. He's got a head injury, so I'd find it very hard to justify to the Police Sergeant why I took his trousers off. And, secondly, I would never wear such an unflattering outfit.'

The children looked at Santa. Nanny Piggins did have a point. Bright red was not very slimming.

'It's almost as if he's proud to have a weight problem!' continued Nanny Piggins. 'In this day and age, when everyone is so concerned about childhood obesity, he is hardly a good role model. No, if I am going to be Santa Claus, I am sure I can find something much more glamorous to wear.'

And so Nanny Piggins dashed upstairs and disappeared into her bedroom. She reappeared five minutes later wearing a fabulous off-the-shoulder crimson ball gown, which was perfectly accessorised by two beautiful earrings that Nanny Piggins had made out of two chocolate Santas. (Chocolate Christmas tree decorations never actually made it to the tree in the Green house.)

'Right, hand me Santa's sack, I'm off to deliver presents,' announced Nanny Piggins.

The children did not know what to say. They could have said 'Are you out of your mind?' or 'How are you going to climb down a chimney dressed in that?' But they realised it would be much more fun watching Nanny Piggins try to climb down a chimney dressed in a ball gown. So Derrick simply said, 'Here you are,' as he handed his nanny the sack. Then they dutifully followed behind her as she carried it out into the street.

'Where shall we deliver presents first?' asked Nanny Piggins.

There were not a lot of children living in the street (one of the chief reasons Mr Green chose to live in the neighbourhood).

'Mrs Roncoli's grandchildren are staying with her,' suggested Samantha. 'Julia is five and Raymond is two.'

'Perfect,' said Nanny Piggins. 'And I know for a fact that Mrs Roncoli baked a Dundee cake this morning so perhaps we can have a slice of cake while we're in there.'

'Wouldn't that be wrong?' asked Derrick.

'We're breaking into her house!' said Nanny Piggins. 'If she catches us, she's not going to quibble about a slice of cake.'

Nanny Piggins, Boris and the children crossed the street and let themselves in through Mrs Roncoli's front gate. Then Boris and the children stood back and watched Nanny Piggins. They should have realised that their nanny was not going to let a little thing like an ankle-length satin ball gown hamper her athleticism. She just hitched the hem of her skirt up into her undies and scampered up the drainpipe like a monkey.

Next it was the children's turn to get up on the roof, and since Derrick, Samantha and Michael had no circus training, this was not so simple. But the children found that if they climbed up Boris and stood on his head (which he did not mind), they were high enough to grasp Nanny Piggins' trotter. Then she could pull them up, one at a time, to join her.

Pulling Boris up was going to be a little bit harder, what with him weighing 700 kilograms and not being able to stand on his own head. But the problem was solved when Nanny Piggins told him she thought she saw a bee by his left foot, and he simply leapt up onto the roof without any help from anyone.

Nanny Piggins, Boris and the children then made their way over to the chimney and peered over the edge. It was very dark and black inside.

'I'm going to throw the presents down first,' said Nanny Piggins, emptying her sack into the chimney. 'That way they can break my fall.'

'Are you sure you wouldn't like us to fetch a rope so we can lower you down?' offered Michael.

'Pish!' said Nanny Piggins as she climbed up on the chimney stack. 'There's no time for that. I have a whole planet's worth of toys to deliver. Wish me luck!' And with one last wave to the children she dived headfirst down the chimney. The children heard nothing for a moment . . . then the distinctive sound of a pig falling headfirst onto a pile of toys.

'Ow!' said Nanny Piggins

'Are you all right?' called Derrick, his voice echoing down the chimney.

'Yes,' replied Nanny Piggins. 'Although in hindsight I probably should have only thrown the soft toys down first. A scale model of the Taj Mahal does not make for a very soft landing.'

'Can you see the Christmas stockings?' asked Michael.

'I can't see anything, it's too dark down here,' said Nanny Piggins. 'No, hang on, I can't see anything because my skirt is over my head. I'll just adjust that . . . Wait a minute, there's no way out! There are bricks on all four sides.'

'I didn't like to say anything earlier, Sarah,' said Boris, leaning over the chimney, 'but Mrs Roncoli did get a gas heater installed last month. You remember, you made the workmen lend you their van so you could get even more chocolate than usual from the sweet shop.'

'What's your point?' asked Nanny Piggins.

'I'm pretty sure that to install a gas heater you first have to brick-up the fireplace,' explained Boris.

'Well of all the . . .' Nanny Piggins muttered a few very rude things that I cannot repeat here in print. But the gist of it was – she was not impressed that Mrs Roncoli had failed to explain the full details of her renovation plans to Nanny Piggins both personally and in writing.

'What are we going to do?' worried Samantha.

'I'm going to give Mrs Roncoli a piece of my mind,' said Nanny Piggins.

'But how are you going to get you out of there?' asked Derrick.

Nanny Piggins looked up at Boris and the children six metres above as they stared down the chimney at her.

'Hmmm,' said Nanny Piggins.

'What are you thinking?' asked Boris.

'I was just thinking . . . that from the inside, a

chimney is an awful lot like a cannon,' said Nanny
Piggins.

Twenty minutes later the children were standing
a safe distance away on the far side of the street as
Boris rolled out the last of the fuse wire.

'This is safe, isn't it?' asked Samantha.

'Well, I wouldn't say it was safe,' admitted Boris
(he was an honest bear). 'If anyone else tried it I'm sure
it would go horribly wrong. But at the circus, Nanny
Piggins used to get blasted out of a cannon seven times
a night, so this will be a walk in the park for her.'

Boris lit the fuse.

'You know we could just knock on Mrs Roncoli's
door and explain what happened,' said Derrick,
beginning to panic.

'Or lower a rope down and pull her out,'
suggested Michael.

'Ooh, that is a good idea,' said Boris. 'It's a shame
it's too late now. Look, the fuse is almost there.'

The children watched in horror as the fuse
disappeared into the chimney.

'Cover your ears,' advised Boris.

Derrick, Samantha and Michael only just put

their hands to their ears before they were shaken by the huge blast. The shockwaves knocked Derrick and Samantha off their feet (it would have knocked Michael off his feet except he was standing right in front of Boris and it is hard to go anywhere when there is a 700 kilogram bear right behind you). Then they saw a streak of crimson rocket up into the sky with the distant cry of 'Yippeeeeeeeeeee!' from Nanny Piggins as she flew up into the strato-sphere.

'Oh my goodness, how is she going to land?!' exclaimed Samantha. 'We didn't rig up a safety net.'

'She'll be fine,' said Boris confidently.

'What do you mean she'll be fine?!' said Derrick. 'Gravity causes a body to accelerate at 9.8 metres per second. If she goes a thousand metres in the air that means she will hit the ground going –' Derrick struggled to do the maths in his head.

'Really fast,' supplied Michael.

'Sarah knows what she is doing,' said Boris.

'Does she secretly have a parachute in her ball gown?' asked Samantha.

'She has got one in her red clutch purse. But whoops!' said Boris, holding up a red clutch purse. 'She gave that to me to mind.'

'Oh no,' said Samantha. 'This is going to be the

worst Christmas ever.' And Samantha knew quite a bit about bad Christmases because their beloved mother had gone missing in mid-December (and before she'd had a chance to make a Christmas cake, so it was a double tragedy).

But a moment later, instead of seeing their nanny plummeting back to earth as they expected, they saw, illuminated in the moonlight, what looked like a giant red umbrella with two pig's feet in the middle, floating slowly down towards the ground.

'I don't believe it!' exclaimed Derrick. 'Nanny Piggins' skirt has puffed out and it's acting as a parachute!'

'Now I can see why Nanny Piggins says it is vitally important to always wear clean underwear,' said Michael.

Nanny Piggins gently drifted down below the line of the rooftops, then they heard the most wonderful sound. Instead of a crash or a thud, there was a huge 'kersplash!' as Nanny Piggins landed safely in the backyard swimming pool of Mr and Mrs Taylor, three blocks away.

'You see, I told you she'd be fine,' said Boris.

Boris and the children ran around to the Taylors' house and met a very soggy Nanny Piggins emerging from the front gate.

'Well that was fun!' said Nanny Piggins excitedly. 'Although I think I've ruined my best ball gown. I must have a word to Mr Taylor about using less chlorine in his pool.'

'You're not hurt?' asked Samantha.

'Not at all,' said Nanny Piggins. 'I enjoyed it tremendously. There was just enough time in my flight for me to eat my chocolate earrings.'

'But what are you going to do about delivering all the toys?' asked Derrick. 'You've been Santa Claus for forty minutes now and you haven't managed to deliver any presents.'

'At this rate you'll never get presents to everyone in just one night,' added Michael.

'I must admit I don't seem to be as effortlessly good at this job as I am at every other job I try,' conceded Nanny Piggins. 'Perhaps we should go and consult Santa. He may have regained consciousness by now, and he might be able to let me in on some of his tricks. He could at least tell me where he parked his reindeer.'

So Nanny Piggins, Boris and the children went back to their house where they found Santa still lying on the couch. They knew he was all right because no-one with a serious head injury would snore that loudly.

'Wake up, Santa,' called Nanny Piggins. 'Wake up!'

Santa suddenly woke up with a grunt and a very unattractive snort. 'What, what, what?' said Santa. 'What is the meaning of this?'

'Santa sounds awfully familiar,' said Samantha, with growing dread.

'Aaaggghhh! His beard has fallen off!' exclaimed Nanny Piggins when Santa's beard came away on her toffee-stained trotters.

But the children were not looking at the beard, they were looking at a far more shocking sight – the now naked-faced Santa.

'Aaaaggghhh, it's Father!' yelled the children.

'Urg,' moaned Mr Green. 'What happened? I've just had the most peculiar dream. I was walking along the street when suddenly a great big fat bear started yelling at me.'

Boris (who had hidden under a lampshade as soon as he saw Mr Green) whimpered. He was very sensitive about his weight.

Nanny Piggins, who was very protective of her brother, slapped Mr Green hard across the face.

'Ow!' squealed Mr Green. 'What did you do that for?'

'Oh I'm sorry,' said Nanny Piggins. 'Slapping

is for hysteria, isn't it? And icepacks are for head injuries. I always get those two confused. I really must finish reading that first-aid book.'

'Give me back my fake beard,' demanded Mr Green. 'I don't want to lose my deposit at the costume shop.'

'I will not. How dare you walk the street impersonating a beloved holiday icon,' scolded Nanny Piggins. 'Children love Santa. Just think how disappointed they would be if they thought Santa was like you.'

'I'm not dressed up in this ridiculous costume voluntarily,' snapped Mr Green. 'I only did it because the Senior Partner made me for the firm's Christmas party.'

'Why you?' asked Derrick.

'I was the only one the red suit would fit,' admitted Mr Green.

'Ah yes, because you're fat,' said Nanny Piggins nodding knowingly.

'But why were you bringing home a big sack full of toys?' asked Michael. 'Shouldn't you have given them out at the Christmas party?'

'I didn't get a chance to give away any toys because none of the children would come and sit on my lap,' grumbled Mr Green. 'I threatened to take a wooden spoon to them if they didn't do as they were told, but that only seemed to make them cry harder.'

'What I want to know,' said Nanny Piggins, 'is if there was a work Christmas party why didn't you take your own children?'

'Um well, um . . .' stuttered Mr Green. 'It never occurred to me. I forgot I had children, I suppose.'

'Well, that's a relief,' said Derrick. 'At least we didn't hurt the real Santa.'

'And we can leave it to the real Santa to deliver presents to all the boys and girls of the world,' added Samantha.

'I suppose,' conceded Nanny Piggins, 'but can we still go back across the road so I can blast myself out of Mrs Roncoli's chimney again. That was a lot of fun.'

'I don't think Mrs Roncoli would appreciate it if we did further structural damage to her home,' worried Samantha.

'Pish!' said Nanny Piggins. 'I'm sure she won't even notice.'

And so Nanny Piggins, Boris and the children had a wonderful Christmas Day. It started well when Mr Green went into the office to do some paper-work (he needed to rack up brownie points because he was going to have a tricky time explaining to the Senior Partner how the sack full of toys had come to be a small pile of melted debris).

Then because Nanny Piggins had never made a Christmas dinner before, the children were in charge of all the cooking. And knowing their nanny well, they served Christmas pudding, Christmas pudding, Christmas pudding and Christmas pudding for entree, main course, dessert and second dessert.

Admittedly Nanny Piggins did ruin the first Christmas pudding. When the children turned off the lights and brought the pudding into the dining room topped with flickering brandy sauce, Nanny Piggins was so horrified to see a dessert on fire she threw herself on the flames (risking her dress and her personal safety).

But once the children had explained that flaming brandy sauce was traditional and in no way damaged the pudding, Nanny Piggins was able to relax and enjoy the meal. She enjoyed sucking the pudding off her dress. And then they all enjoyed eating the other three puddings off plates. After they had eaten as much as was physically possible, they went into the living room and had a wonderful time watching Boris perform *The Nutcracker*. (He did break two vases and the light fitting but only because he put on such a spectacular performance.)

'So, Nanny Piggins,' said Michael, 'what do you think of Christmas?'

'I think it's wonderful,' said Nanny Piggins.

'Does that mean you're not going to put chicken wire over the chimney next year then?' asked Derrick.

'No, of course not,' said Nanny Piggins.

'Good,' said Samantha with relief.

'Next year,' said Nanny Piggins, 'I'll put a trip wire down by the stockings. Santa will never see that coming.'

CHAPTER 10

Nanny Piggins Turns a Lemon into Lemonade

'It's just not good enough!' bellowed Nanny Piggins.

'I'm asking you to leave!' countered the librarian.

'Hah!' said Nanny Piggins. 'This is a public library. I am a member of the public. You can't throw me out!'

'You are disturbing everyone,' admonished the librarian.

Nanny Piggins turned and addressed the handful of sad souls with nowhere better to go than a public library on a Friday afternoon. 'Do you mind me disturbing you?'

They all shook their heads. They were enjoying Nanny Piggins' argument with the librarian immensely. It is true that the librarian was a good woman, a lover of literature and very conscientious. But it is a sad fact of human nature that if you hand out enough twenty-cent fines for overdue books, you develop enemies. So watching Nanny Piggins berate the librarian was a pleasure for the library regulars – it was something that they had secretly been wishing they could do for years.

'We cannot have the entire library devoted solely to romance novels and cookbooks,' protested the librarian.

'Why not?!' demanded Nanny Piggins. 'You'd get a lot more customers. Or is that the problem? If you actually had customers there would be less time for you to sneak off to the break room and secretly scoff biscuits while reading the latest romance novels before you put them out on the shelves.'

The librarian blushed. (She did like biscuits and she did secretly read all the romance novels before she put them out. It was hard work finding time in the day to then go home and read all the literature books as well. She really could not be expected to stamp books and speak to members of the public when she had so much to do.)

'Maybe we should go, Nanny Piggins,' suggested Samantha. She had just borrowed the latest Tracey McWeldon book and while she would enjoy seeing her nanny wrestle with the librarian, she was anxious to get the book home without it being taken from her in a fit of retribution by the librarian.

'All right,' said Nanny Piggins, still glaring at the librarian. 'Although I still maintain it should be a crime to have all these books and yet provide no snacks. How can you enjoy reading without eating cake?'

'That's another thing!' accused the librarian, getting up a head of steam. She was starting to enjoy the argument now. (The one-metre-wide library counter was giving her a false sense of confidence. She did not realise how athletic Nanny Piggins was, or how quickly her adversary could vault it.) 'Every time you return books they are covered in cake crumbs, chocolate and icing!'

'For which you should thank me!' declared Nanny Piggins. 'The next reader is welcome to lick it off. I believe in sharing.'

'Right, that's it!' said the librarian, snatching up Nanny Piggins' library card. 'I am banning you from the library!' She cut the library card in two.

The children gasped.

Nanny Piggins' eyes bulged. She did not know what to do first. Bite the librarian or rush back into the library and lick all the books she had ever borrowed herself.

'You shouldn't have done that,' sighed Derrick.

Fortunately for the librarian, at that very moment the Police Sergeant entered.

'Ah, Police Sergeant,' said the librarian, 'I'm so glad you have arrived. Please see this pig off the premises.'

'Oh, okay,' said the Police Sergeant.

He was not there because of the disturbance. No-one had called the police because even the other library staff were enjoying the scene too much to want it to end. The Police Sergeant had come to the library to secretly borrow detective novels (he picked up quite a lot of pointers that way). But on seeing the murderous glare Nanny Piggins was giving the librarian, he realised he would not be borrowing any books that day.

Unlike the librarian, the Police Sergeant had plenty of experience dealing with Nanny Piggins so he knew just how to speak to her. 'Nanny Piggins, it is so good to see you. You look lovely today,' said the Police Sergeant politely. 'Would you be so kind as to step out to the patrol car with me?'

Nanny Piggins glowered at him.

'I have a packet of chocolate biscuits in the glove box,' continued the Police Sergeant.

No-one actually saw Nanny Piggins leave the building because she flew out of the library so fast. By the time the children joined her she was sitting in the passenger seat chatting with the young Police Constable, eating chocolate biscuits and trying to persuade him to let her turn on the police siren.

The Police Sergeant was then kind enough to drive them all home. He even let Nanny Piggins wear his police hat and turn on the siren while he drove through a few red lights (he did not need much persuading, he enjoyed doing that himself). So when they arrived back at the Green house, Nanny Piggins was not as grumpy as she might have been about being banned from the local library. Although she had borrowed the Police Constable's pen and notebook to write a little note reminding herself to get revenge on the librarian next time there was a rainy day or she had some spare time to fill.

So Nanny Piggins and the children waved goodbye to the police officers, then let themselves in, which was when the second unpleasant event of the day occurred. They opened the door and found Mr Green waiting for them with a strained smile on his face and a large chocolate cake in his hands.

'Hello, Nanny Piggins,' said Mr Green through clenched teeth (he was not very good at smiling, he had so little practice).

'What's this?' asked Nanny Piggins suspiciously, sniffing first the cake, then Mr Green, to try to determine what was going on.

'Nothing,' said Mr Green. 'I just thought I'd buy a nice cake for my favourite nanny. You'd like a cake, wouldn't you?' asked Mr Green, offering it to her.

Nanny Piggins backed away. 'This isn't right. What's going on?' demanded Nanny Piggins. 'Is the cake poisoned? Have I been poisoned?! Are you giving me a cake because you know I only have thirty minutes to live?!'

'Not at all,' said Mr Green, with the false smile still plastered across his face. 'I'm giving you a cake because I like you.'

'Quick! Run, children!' ordered Nanny Piggins. 'Your father has obviously lost his mind.'

'Just take the darn cake,' snapped Mr Green, unable to keep up the pretence of being nice any longer. 'Can't you see I'm trying to bribe you?'

'Oooooh,' said Nanny Piggins, suddenly catching on. 'Well that does make a refreshing change. My not having to tell you to bribe me. I'm glad to see you taking the initiative for once.'

'Well done, Father,' congratulated Derrick.

'So what is it you want?' asked Nanny Piggins, taking the cake, biting off a big mouthful and sharing the rest with the children.

'It's the Father of the Year Competition,' said Mr Green.

Nanny Piggins and the children groaned.

'Not that again?' complained Nanny Piggins. 'What do you want me to do this time? Teach the children to dance about, singing in five-part harmony?'

'There are only three of us,' pointed out Michael.

'Yes, that would make it particularly difficult,' agreed Nanny Piggins. 'Still, I suppose we could adopt Samson and Margaret. It would only be fair – someone really should liberate them from Nanny Anne.'

'No, no, no,' interrupted Mr Green. 'It's nothing like that. It was announced today that there are three finalists in the company's Father of the Year Competition . . .'

'Oh, never mind,' comforted Nanny Piggins kindly. 'At least you tried.'

'You don't understand,' said Mr Green. 'I am one of the finalists.'

Nanny Piggins and the children were shocked. (Nanny Piggins would have spat out her mouthful of cake in surprise, but it was a particularly delicious one, so she did not.)

'But how is that possible?!' exclaimed Nanny Piggins. 'The Senior Partner has seen you interacting with the children.'

'Well, apparently, if you take a whole law firm full of lawyers, it is very hard to find three of them who are good fathers,' said Mr Green. 'Smythe from Accounting actually knew all his children's birthdays and most of their names, so obviously he went straight through. And Harris from Maritime Law was seen taking his four-year-old to the park on his own without a woman there to help him, so he automatically got picked as well. Luckily Peterson still hasn't been released by the tribe in Papua New Guinea. Apparently they think he is a god just because he's been giving them good stock-market tips.'

'But why on earth did they choose you?' asked Nanny Piggins.

Mr Green looked shifty and did not answer.

'You'd better tell her, Father,' encouraged Derrick. 'You know she'll find out anyway, and you won't like the way she does it.'

'All right,' snapped Mr Green grumpily. 'The Senior Partner said that while I was terrible in all other respects, I had made one stroke of genius.'

'Which was?' asked Samantha.

'Hrrring nnn pggg,' mumbled Mr Green, trying not to make eye contact.

'I'm sorry, we didn't quite catch that?' said Michael.

'The Senior Partner said I made a stroke of genius when I hired Nanny Piggins,' confessed Mr Green.

Nanny Piggins smiled. 'I always thought your new Senior Partner was a lovely, insightful man.'

'So why are you giving Nanny Piggins a cake?' asked Samantha. 'To thank her?'

'Of course not,' said Mr Green as though this was the most ridiculous suggestion in the world. 'No, you see, there is a final stage in the competition to find out who the ultimate winner is.'

'You mean who the best father is,' said Derrick.

'Yes, yes, same difference,' said Mr Green. 'Anyway, the Senior Partner has set us a task. We have to team up with our children and raise money for charity. Whoever raises the most money wins.'

'Right,' said Nanny Piggins.

'So could you do all that for me?' said Mr Green, picking up his briefcase and straightening his tie. 'I want to get back to the office.'

'Wait just a minute!' said Nanny Piggins, blocking his path. 'It is called the "Father of the Year Competition", not the "Nanny of the Year Competition".'

'They'd never have a competition like that,' said Michael. 'You'd win hands down every year.'

'True,' agreed Nanny Piggins. 'But my point is, if you want to win, then you should jolly well do some fathering yourself.'

'But, but, but . . .' whined Mr Green, 'I don't want to.'

'Tough,' said Nanny Piggins. 'I do everything else for you. I can't be you for you as well.'

'But I don't know how to arrange a charity event,' complained Mr Green.

'Then you'd better learn,' said Nanny Piggins. 'Here, take back your cake. I refuse to accept your bribe.' (The strength of this gesture was somewhat diminished by the fact that it was already three-quarters eaten.)

'Fine,' snapped Mr Green. 'I order you three children to meet me at 7 am tomorrow morning for a breakfast meeting to discuss what we are going to do.' With that, Mr Green got in his Rolls Royce and returned to his office.

'Nanny Piggins, what have you done?' asked Michael. 'We have to go to a meeting!'

'And at 7 am on a Saturday!' exclaimed Derrick.

'And with Father!' exclaimed Samantha (which was the most horrific kind of 7 am Saturday breakfast meeting she could imagine).

'You are going to get us out of it, aren't you?' asked Michael.

Nanny Piggins looked at the three children. It broke her heart to see their crestfallen little faces. But she had principles.

'I'm not,' said Nanny Piggins. 'I am sorry that you are going to have to suffer this, when you have suffered so much already: the loss of your mother, the cruelties of compulsory education and, on occasion, having to eat vegetables. But there are some points on which a pig should stand firm. Your father should spend some time with you. And while that may be deeply unpleasant for you, sometimes you have to suffer unpleasantness to do what is right.'

'We do?' asked Michael.

'Oh yes,' said Nanny Piggins. 'Look at Superman. He is the strongest, most powerful man in the universe. And yet he still has to wear his underpants on the outside of his leotard. We all have our crosses to bear. You will just have to be strong and see it through. And if your father is too unbearable, let me know and I will come and bite his leg for you.'

The following two weeks were not pleasant for the Green children. Admittedly, they did not have to spend too much time with their father. He soon discovered he could organise the event simply by ringing up and barking orders at them on the phone. But the children were surprised when Nanny Piggins actually stayed true to her word and left them to it. They thought she would not be able to resist sweeping in and transforming the drab event Mr Green was organising into something fabulous.

When the big night arrived the children trooped into the living room to say goodbye to her. Nanny Piggins was curled up in an armchair, eating a box of chocolates and reading a very silly novel (about how the truth about the Loch Ness monster was hidden in coded messages painted into Salvador Dali paintings).

'So you're really not coming with us?' asked Derrick.

'I'm afraid not,' said Nanny Piggins. 'I do hope it is not too awful for you. But if it is, always remember – what's my first rule about awkward social situations?'

'Trip the fire alarm,' chorused the children.

'And what's the best way to trip the fire alarm?' coached Nanny Piggins.

'By setting a fire,' chanted the children.

'That's right,' said Nanny Piggins approvingly. 'I can't tell you how many tedious tupperware parties that has got me out of.'

'It wouldn't be so awful if you came with us,' pleaded Michael.

'Even if you just sat in the corner and said mean things about people's haircuts, it would really cheer us up,' added Derrick

'I know,' said Nanny Piggins, giving them each a hug. 'But you really do need to interact with your father. Once a year or so, and obviously not for very long. Just remember, while it may not feel that way at the time, very few people actually die of boredom.'

And so, after Nanny Piggins had pressed half-a-dozen chocolate bars into each of their pockets and kissed them goodbye, the children left to go to their father's horrible function.

Nanny Piggins was surprised when, just forty-five minutes, two engrossing chapters and twelve chocolate bars later, the children returned.

'What are you doing back already?' asked Nanny Piggins. 'And you're not even wet from the sprinkler system. Let me guess – your father held his function at a venue with inadequate fire protection?'

'No, better than that!' said Samantha.

'Nobody turned up,' explained Derrick.

'Nobody?' asked Nanny Piggins.

'Nobody at all,' said Michael with a grin.

'What sort of social function did your father organise?' asked Nanny Piggins. 'Even street performers who can barely hack their way through a three-chord song can get people to give them the loose change from their pockets.'

'Father decided he didn't want to do a sit-down

dinner because the food costs were too expensive,' explained Samantha.

'So it was just out-of-date crackers with the cheapest lump of cheddar he could find,' continued Derrick.

'And he didn't want to pay a professional performer to entertain the audience,' added Michael, 'so he was going to give a speech himself.'

'No!' gasped Nanny Piggins. 'What about? Was he going to give a lecture on how to be boring?'

'Close,' conceded Samantha. 'He was going to give a talk explaining lesser known details of the law as it applies to offshore trust funds.'

'I'm surprised there weren't insomniacs beating down the door, begging to attend,' said Nanny Piggins. 'That would be guaranteed to put anyone to sleep.'

'Well, there might have been,' admitted Derrick, 'but you know how father feels about advertising.'

'Let me guess,' said Nanny Piggins. 'All he did was paint a sign himself and stab it in the ground outside the hall?'

'Exactly,' said Samantha.

'Oh well, at least that ordeal was nowhere as bad as we all thought it would be,' said Nanny Piggins. 'And the Father of the Year Competition will be all over in a couple of days, so you won't have to spend time with your father again for months, if not years, provided you are very careful and don't get caught in an elevator with him.' Nanny Piggins shuddered. 'What a horrific thought! I highly recommend you never ever get in an elevator with your father, just to be on the safe side.'

The children also shuddered at the nightmare-like idea.

'Come on, let's do something fun,' said Nanny Piggins. 'The retired army colonel who lives round the corner has just bought himself a ferret. Let's go round and play with it.'

'But it's 9 pm,' protested Derrick.

'He won't mind being suddenly woken up,' said Nanny Piggins. 'It'll remind him of the war.'

But just then their pleasant plans were ruined when they heard Mr Green coming in through the front door.

'Darn,' said Nanny Piggins. 'I suppose bopping him on the head and going out anyway would be rude.'

'I don't know much about etiquette,' said Samantha, 'but it certainly sounds like that would be a rude thing to do.'

Nanny Piggins and the children went out into

the hallway to greet Mr Green (and then try to escape around him at the first opportunity).

'Sorry to hear that your evening went so poorly,' said Nanny Piggins. 'Still, at least you won't have to buy any cheese and crackers for a while, hey?'

But Mr Green was not very good at looking on the bright side of anything. He was, by nature, a 'glass half-empty' man. So he responded to Nanny Piggins' attempt at joviality by bursting into tears.

Nanny Piggins and the children were horrified as Mr Green covered his eyes, sobbed loudly and lurched towards them, as if wanting a hug. They instinctively backed away.

'What should we do?' asked Derrick.

'Is this part of our compulsory father inter-action?' asked Samantha.

'No, it has gone beyond that, the situation is officially out of control,' declared Nanny Piggins. 'This is more responsibility than any child should have to bear. Don't worry, I will take care of it.'

'You're not going to hug him, are you?' asked Michael, clutching Nanny Piggins' hand and not wanting to let her go.

'I can handle it,' Nanny Piggins assured him.

She carefully edged towards Mr Green, reached out an arm and patted him on the back.

'There, there, Mr Green, it will be all right,' said Nanny Piggins. 'If you haven't taken the cheese out of its packet, perhaps you'll be able to return it.'

'That's not it,' wailed Mr Green. 'I'm upset because I just found out the prize for the Father of the Year Competition was an all-expenses-paid, two-week family trip to Hawaii. And if I'd cashed in the children's tickets and gone on my own, I would have been able to have such a lovely time.'

The children gasped. Now they were devastated too. They were imagining what a wonderful time they would have had with their father gone for two weeks.

'Then you're just going to have to win that prize!' announced Nanny Piggins.

'But it's too late,' blubbered Mr Green. 'The competition ends on Monday. And I'm twenty dollars in deficit.'

'Leave it to me,' said Nanny Piggins.

'But I thought you said that the purpose of the Father of the Year Competition was for us to spend time with Father,' said Michael.

'It's all very well to have principles. But sometimes there are more important things at stake. Like a two-week holiday from having your father about the house,' said Nanny Piggins. 'You go back to the office, Mr Green. I will take care of it all.'

'Oh thank you, thank you so much,' gushed Mr Green. For a moment it looked like he was going to hug Nanny Piggins from sheer gratitude, but he immediately thought better of it and fled the house.

'What are you going to do, Nanny Piggins?' asked Derrick.

'Smythe has raised $8000 by doing a sponsored walk around the block one thousand times,' said Samantha.

'And Harris has raised $11,000 by auctioning off paintings done by badgers,' said Michael.

'Piffle!' said Nanny Piggins. 'I'm sure I can do better than that.'

The next morning when the children came down to breakfast they were surprised to discover their nanny hard at work in the kitchen.

'What are you doing, Nanny Piggins?' asked Samantha.

'There is an old saying,' explained Nanny Piggins. 'When life gives you a lemon, make lemonade.'

'When did life give you a lemon?' asked Michael, looking at the hundreds of squeezed lemons lying on the kitchen counter.

'It didn't,' admitted Nanny Piggins. 'I borrowed these from Mrs McGill's lemon tree. But the principle is still the same. Making lemonade is an excellent way to solve all your problems.'

'It is?' asked Derrick sceptically.

'Oh yes,' said Nanny Piggins.

'How?' asked Samantha.

'We are going to set up a lemonade stand,' explained Nanny Piggins.

'But it's not even a hot day outside,' said Michael, looking out the window at the overcast sky.

'Pish!' said Nanny Piggins.

As if a little thing like that would stop her.

Half an hour later they were all sitting behind a makeshift table, with a jug of lemonade and a few plastic cups. Nanny Piggins was humming happily to herself. But the children were not so confident that this was a high stakes money-making scheme.

'Do you think you are going to get many

customers?' asked Samantha. 'There aren't many people about this morning.'

'I'm confident I'll get at least one,' said Nanny Piggins smugly.

'Why? What have you done?' asked Derrick, beginning to feel suspicious.

'I don't know what you mean,' said Nanny Piggins, unable to keep the smirk off her face. 'Ah, here comes Boris now. And look at that. He seems to have brought a friend.'

The children turned to see Boris walking towards them and he appeared to be carrying a struggling man. They could not hear exactly what the man was yelling because his face was pressed into Boris' back, but they could tell from his tone that he was not happy.

'Ppp-mm-dwn,' yelled the man.

'In a second,' said Boris kindly. 'I know being kidnapped is not a lot of fun. It has happened to me several times. But I promise you, you'll think it is entirely worthwhile in this instance.'

'Hello, Boris,' called Nanny Piggins. 'Bring him over here.'

'Hello, Sarah,' replied Boris. 'I'm glad to see you. He's quite a wiggler, even after I explained it would be easier for me to carry him if he just lay still.'

Boris set the man down on his feet.

'This is an outrage!' spluttered the angry man. 'I'm calling the police.'

'Good idea,' said Nanny Piggins. 'I'm sure the Police Sergeant would like a glass of lemonade.'

'I'm a busy man, I don't have time to be kidnapped,' shouted the angry man.

'Of course you don't,' said Nanny Piggins kindly. 'You must be very hot and bothered after your ordeal. Here, have a free glass of lemonade.'

'But, Nanny Piggins,' whispered Michael. 'How are we going to make money if you give the lemonade away?'

'And how are we going to make money if we are all arrested for kidnapping?' added Derrick.

'Trust me,' whispered Nanny Piggins, holding out the cup to the angry man.

'All right, I will have some,' said the angry man. (A face full of bear fur does tend to make you thirsty.) So he took the cup and gulped it down.

But when he lowered the cup, the angry man did not continue yelling as the children had expected. He had a very different look on his face – it combined excitement, concentration and business acumen.

'What is in that lemonade?' the man asked shrewdly.

'I won't tell you,' said Nanny Piggins.

'It is the most delicious lemonade I have ever tasted,' said the man.

'I know,' agreed Nanny Piggins.

'How much do you want for the recipe?' asked the man.

'It's not for sale,' declared Nanny Piggins. 'It's a family recipe that has been passed down from generation to generation.'

'I am the chairman of the world's largest soft-drink company,' said the angry man.

'Really?' said Nanny Piggins, a little too innocently. 'What a surprise.'

The children looked at their nanny. They were beginning to suspect that she had put more thought into her kidnapping plot than they had realised.

'You have to sell me the recipe,' pleaded the angry man. 'This lemonade is going to be a huge hit. I'll give you whatever you want.'

'I don't know,' said Nanny Piggins. 'Great-Great-Aunt Hilda would turn over in her grave if she knew I'd sold it.'

The man was now starting to get desperate, 'One million dollars? Two million dollars?! I have to have that recipe.'

Nanny Piggins turned to the children. 'How much did Harris from Maritime Law make?'

'Eleven thousand dollars,' said Michael.

Nanny Piggins turned back to the soft drink chairman. 'We want $11,000 *and* fifty cents,' declared Nanny Piggins.

'But Nanny Piggins,' said Derrick, 'he just offered you two million dollars. Why don't you take that?'

'Oh no, I'm not a greedy pig,' said Nanny Piggins. 'We want your father to look good, but not that good.'

And so, when Mr Green set out for work on Monday morning, his chest swelled with pride. Not because he had spent time with his children, or because he had raised money for charity. But because he had thrashed Smythe from Accounting and Harris from Maritime Law, which, to his mind, was much more important than family values or charitable organisations.

There was to be a presentation ceremony when he arrived at work. Nanny Piggins and the children went with him – partly to see him win the Father of the Year Competition, but mainly to make sure he got his trip to Hawaii. They had such plans for the fortnight they were going to spend without him.

When they got to the law firm all the employees were gathered in the car park, a small stage had been set up, and a crystal 'Father of the Year' trophy was on a plinth, waiting to be presented. Mr Green made his way through the crowd, loudly saying things like, 'Out of the way, Father of the Year coming through.' Then he climbed up on stage and waited for the Senior Partner to arrive and give him his award.

He waited.

And waited.

Nine o'clock bled into 9.15, then 9.30. At ten o'clock employees began to make their way back inside. But Mr Green still stood on the stage waiting. This was his moment in the sun. He did not care if no-one was there to witness it. He just wanted his tickets to Hawaii.

Eventually a tear-stained secretary came out and climbed up on the stage.

'What are you doing here?' asked Mr Green. 'This is no place for secretaries. I'm waiting for the Senior Partner.'

'He isn't coming,' sobbed the secretary. 'He's run off.'

'What?' exploded Mr Green.

'He's embezzled all the charity money and flown off overseas,' said the secretary. 'And he never even said goodbye . . .' She broke down sobbing at this point (because naturally she had fallen in love with the Senior Partner).

'The Senior Partner is a conman?!' exclaimed Derrick.

'And a thief?!' exclaimed Samantha.

'Cool!' exclaimed Michael.

'I suspected it all along,' said Nanny Piggins. 'He winked and smiled too much to be a real lawyer.'

'But what about my prize?' asked Mr Green.

'It was all just a hoax,' said the secretary. 'He isn't a qualified lawyer. He never even went to a job interview. He just turned up the morning after Isabella Dunkhurst left, announced he was the new Senior Partner, and everyone believed him.'

'Do I at least get the trophy?' asked Mr Green.

'No, you do not,' said a stern voice behind them.

They all spun round and behold! Standing there was none other than the world's first tap-dancing lawyer herself, Isabella Dunkhurst. But she was not wearing her tap shoes and leopard-print leotard now, she was back in her corporate uniform, a grey power suit. 'The trophy has to go back to the shop because it has not been paid for,' declared the former Senior Partner.

'You're back!' exclaimed Mr Green. Now he had tears in his eyes too, but his were tears of joy.

'Yes,' said Isabella Dunkhurst. 'It seems I can't leave the firm for five minutes without the whole thing being taken over by a confidence trickster.'

'But what about your dancing career?' asked Nanny Piggins.

'It's going very well,' said Isabella Dunkhurst, 'but I have to take six months off anyway. I've got a stress fracture in my big toe from tapping so hard.'

Boris nodded. 'It is so important to build up the strength in your arches before you go profes-sional.' (Mr Green did not notice Boris because he was holding a hubcap in front of his face to disguise himself as a car.)

'But my prize?' whimpered Mr Green.

'Pull yourself together, Mr Green,' said Nanny Piggins sternly. 'You didn't do anything to deserve your prize, so you've got no right to complain now that it's gone.'

'But what about our two-week holiday from Father?' asked Derrick.

'Oh I'm sure we can still manage that,' said Nanny Piggins. 'There's a new futon shop in town. We can buy him one and then ask Ms Dunkhurst to let him sleep in the office for a couple of weeks.'

Actually, apart from the disappointment of not getting to go to Hawaii, Mr Green was pretty pleased with how everything turned out. He was delighted to have Isabella Dunkhurst back. She tore strips off him for stealing tea bags from the break room and he enjoyed every moment of it. It was such a relief to be able to relax and just be himself (a bad father). And it was a relief for Nanny Piggins and the children to not have him trying to be nice and spend time with them.

Later that week, as Nanny Piggins and the children were sitting around the table having breakfast, Boris entered, carrying a parcel.

'This just arrived for you,' said Boris, handing it to Nanny Piggins.

'Oh goody!' said Nanny Piggins. 'It's probably the scorpion I wrote and asked Eduardo to send us for Samantha's assignment.'

'But I handed in that assignment months ago,' said Samantha.

'Sadly the Mexican postal system is even less reliable than our own,' explained Nanny Piggins as she opened the box. But when she looked inside there were no scorpions, spiders or even venomous snakes.

'What's this?' asked Nanny Piggins. 'It looks like a trophy.'

A note fell to the floor and Samantha picked it up. 'It's from the Senior Partner!'

'What?!' exclaimed Nanny Piggins. 'But he's on the run! Why would he be writing to me?'

The children all gathered round to read the note. It said:

> *Dear Nanny Piggins,*
>
> *This trophy is for you. None of those men deserved a 'Father of the Year Award' but you deserve this.*
>
> *Yours Sincerely,*
>
> *Senior Partner (sorry I can't tell you my real name)*
>
> *xxoo*

Nanny Piggins pulled the trophy out of the parcel. It said:

This
Nanny of the Millennium Award
goes to
Sarah Matahari Lorelai Piggins
for her loving service to child care,
above and beyond the call of duty.

Nanny Piggins rubbed her eyes. 'You know, for a despicable thieving conman, he wasn't such a bad chap.'

Derrick, Samantha and Michael gave their nanny a big hug. They were just sad that it took an amoral conman and not their own father to recognise what a wonderful nanny Nanny Piggins really was.

ABOUT THE AUTHOR

R.A. Spratt is an award-winning comedy writer with fourteen years' experience in the television industry. She lives in Sydney with her husband and two daughters. Unlike Nanny Piggins, she has never willingly been blasted out of a cannon.

To find more, visit www.raspratt.com